He tasted her. He claimed. He—

"The cop was still here," Cooper growled against her lips. "I didn't want him suspicious."

He was kissing her for a cover.

Had she moaned? She'd definitely sunk her nails into his shoulders. She'd even arched against him.

"I...I know," she lied. Their mouths were barely an inch apart. "The kiss was a good idea."

A car cranked. The engine growled.

"I'm guessing that's him," Gabrielle said as she kept her hands on Cooper. But she did retract her nails. "Pulling away?"

He nodded. "I'm not letting you go until he's gone."

THE GIRL NEXT DOOR

New York Times **Bestselling Author**

CYNTHIA EDEN

Thank you so much to the fabulous staff at Harlequin Books. Working with you is a pleasure!

ISBN-13: 978-0-373-74801-3

THE GIRL NEXT DOOR

This edition published by arrangement with Harlequin Books S.A.

For questions and comments about the quality of this book, please contact us at CustomerService@Harlequin.com.

Printed in U.S.A.

ABOUT THE AUTHOR

New York Times and *USA TODAY* bestselling author Cynthia Eden writes tales of romantic suspense and paranormal romance. Her books have received starred reviews from *Publishers Weekly,* and she has received a RITA® Award nomination for best romantic suspense novel. Cynthia lives in the Deep South, loves horror movies and has an addiction to chocolate. More information about Cynthia may be found on her website, www.cynthiaeden.com, or you can follow her on Twitter (www.twitter.com/cynthiaeden).

Books by Cynthia Eden

HARLEQUIN INTRIGUE

1398—ALPHA ONE*
1404—GUARDIAN RANGER*
1437—SHARPSHOOTER*
1445—GLITTER AND GUNFIRE*
1474—UNDERCOVER CAPTOR**
1480—THE GIRL NEXT DOOR**

*Shadow Agents
**Shadow Agents: Guts and Glory

CAST OF CHARACTERS

Gabrielle Harper—Reporter Gabrielle Harper is working on the biggest case of her career. But while she's tracking a killer, Gabrielle finds herself *becoming* the story. Desperate and afraid, she turns to her neighbor Cooper Marshall for help. Only, Cooper isn't the man she believes him to be....

Cooper Marshall—This former U.S. Air Force pararescueman has spent most of his life literally jumping into danger. Now he spends his days completing covert work for the Elite Operations Division. When Gabrielle asks for his help, she believes that she is hiring a P.I. Cooper's sexy neighbor has no clue that she's just gotten a special agent bodyguard.

Hugh Keller—Gabrielle's boss at the *Inquisitor,* Hugh is a man who knows all of the dark secrets that wait in the D.C. shadows. But when threats hit too close to home, even Hugh may not be able to help Gabrielle, the woman he thinks of as his daughter.

Bruce Mercer—The director of the EOD doesn't like to bring civilians into the danger that his agents face each day, but when Gabrielle gets caught in the cross fire, he has no choice. One of the EOD's own agents has gone rogue, and that agent is hunting Gabrielle.

Dylan Foxx—As always, Dylan is ready to back up his teammates. He'll walk willingly into any danger, and he'll face the monsters that wait in the dark. Dylan knows that this case is personal—an EOD agent has gone rogue. He isn't going to stop his search until the traitor is unmasked.

Rachel Mancini—Rachel knows how to control her fear and get the job done. But as she hunts for a killer who is hiding in plain sight, she wonders if it is truly safe to trust the team that surrounds her.

Lane Carmichael—The D.C. detective has a past with Gabrielle. He doesn't trust Cooper, and as the body count rises in the city, he finds himself heading straight into a face-off with a killer.

Chapter One

Cooper Marshall burst into the apartment, gun ready as his gaze swept the dim interior of the room that waited for him. "Lockwood!"

There was no response to his call, but the stench in the air—that unmistakable odor of death and blood—told Cooper that he'd arrived too late.

Again.

Damn it.

Cooper rushed deeper into that darkened apartment. He'd gotten his orders from the top. He'd been assigned to track down Keith Lockwood, an ex–Elite Operations Division agent. Cooper was supposed to confirm that the other man was alive and well. He'd fallen off the EOD's radar, and that had sure raised a red flag in the mind of Cooper's boss.

Especially since other EOD agents had recently turned up dead.

Cooper rounded a corner in the narrow hallway. The scent of blood was stronger. He headed toward what he suspected was the bedroom. His eyes had already adjusted to the darkness, so it was easy for him to see the body slumped on the floor just a few feet from him.

He knelt, and his gloved fingers turned the body just slightly. Cooper pulled out his penlight and shone it on the dead man's face.

Keith Lockwood. Cooper had never worked with the man on a mission, but he'd seen Lockwood's photos.

Lockwood's throat had been slit. An up-close kill.

Considering that Lockwood was a former navy SEAL, the man shouldn't have been caught off guard.

But he had been.

Because the killer isn't your average thug off the streets.

The killer was also an agent with the EOD, and the killer was trained just as well as Lockwood had been.

No, trained *better.*

Because the killer had been able to get the drop on the SEAL.

Cooper's breath eased out in a rough sigh just as a knock sounded on the front door.

The front door that Cooper had just smashed open moments before.

He leapt to his feet.

"Mr. Lockwood?" A feminine voice called out. "Mr. Lockwood…i-is everything all right?"

No, things were far from *all right.* The broken door *should* have been a dead giveaway on that point.

"It's Gabrielle Harper!" The voice called out. "We were supposed to meet…"

His back teeth clenched. Talk about extremely bad timing. He knew Gabrielle Harper, and the trouble that the woman was about to bring his way was just going to make the situation even more of a tangled mess.

Cooper holstered his weapon. He had to get out of that apartment. *Before* Gabrielle saw him and asked questions that he couldn't answer for her.

He rose and stalked toward the bedroom window. His footsteps were silent. After all of his training, they should have been.

Gabrielle's steps—and her high heels—tapped across the hardwood floor as she came inside the apartment.

Of course, Gabrielle wasn't just going to wait outside. She was a reporter, no doubt on the scent of a story.

And she must have scented the blood.

She was following that scent, and if he didn't move, fast, she'd follow it straight to him.

Cooper opened the window then glanced down below. Three floors up. But there were bricks on the side of the building, with crevices in between them. If he held on just right, he could spider-crawl his way down.

The floor in the hallway creaked as Gabrielle paused.

She should have called for help by now. At the first sign of that smashed door, Gabrielle should have dialed 911. But, with Gabrielle what she *should* do and what she actually *did*—well, those could be very different things.

If she wasn't careful, the woman was going to walk into real trouble one day—the kind that she wouldn't be able to walk away from.

He slid through the window. Since it was after midnight, Cooper knew he'd virtually disappear into the darkness when he climbed down the back side of the building.

He'd make it out of there, undetected, provided he didn't fall and break his neck.

He eased to the side, his feet resting against the window's narrow ledge. He pulled the window back down and took a deep breath.

"Mr. Lockwood!" Gabrielle's horror-filled scream broke loud and clear through the night.

She'd found the body.

Jaw locking, Cooper made his way down that building.

Gabrielle had just stumbled into an extremely

dangerous situation. Now he'd have to do some serious recon in order to keep her out of the cross fire.

IT WASN'T HER first dead body.

Gabrielle Harper stood behind the patrol car, her gaze on the apartment building. The cops had rolled in quickly after her call then they'd pushed her *out*.

They hadn't needed to push her so far. She knew better than to contaminate the scene. They didn't have to worry about her destroying evidence.

Not my first dead body. But the sight of Lockwood's slit throat had still made nausea rise within her.

"Tell me again," Detective Lane Carmichael said as he leaned back against the patrol car and studied her with an assessing gaze, "just why you were at Keith Lockwood's house in the middle of the night?"

A crowd had already gathered.

Her gaze slid away from Lane's and toward the apartment's entrance. The body was being wheeled out through the double doors. Lockwood had been zipped up in a black bag. Bagged, tagged and taken away.

She swallowed.

"Gabrielle."

The snap of her name jerked her attention back

to Lane. His suit was wrinkled, his dark hair was tousled and his face was set in grim, I'm-sure-not-pleased-with-you lines.

That was typically the way Lane looked at her. Even when they'd been dating—briefly—he'd often given her that same look.

She worked the crime beat in Washington, D.C., covering stories for the *Inquisitor*—both the paper and its online subscriber base. Since Lane was a homicide detective, their paths crossed plenty.

That crossing had been good when they were dating.

Now that they weren't—not so good.

"Lockwood called me," she began.

"Dead men don't make phone calls." His arms were crossed over his chest—his interrogation stance. "The ME estimates that he's been dead for over seven hours. Try again."

Seven hours. She filed that helpful detail away for later. "He called me around eight a.m. The guy left a voice message for me, saying he had some info to share about a story I'd covered."

Lane's head tilted. "Just what story would that be?"

Gabrielle pushed back her hair. It was summer in D.C., and she was sweating. "The unsolved murder of Kylie Archer." A woman whose body had been discovered in her apartment months ago. Kylie's throat had been slit.

Just like Lockwood's.

Even in the summer heat goose bumps rose on her arms.

"I need everything you've got on Lockwood, Gabby," Lane told her, his voice grim. "Everything."

But she could only shake her head. The body had been loaded into the coroner's van. Uniforms began to walk back into the apartment building. "I don't have anything to give you. He called *me.* Left a message for me to meet him at this address after midnight. He mentioned Kylie's name and said he had more information for me." She was trying to cooperate, didn't Lane get that? "I'd just run a piece on the web, highlighting Kylie's unsolved murder, so I figured that Lockwood had seen it and he had a lead to share with me."

Once a month, she featured an unsolved crime in her column. Thanks to those features, she'd helped close three cold cases.

Lane should thank her for that help.

His glare said he wouldn't be thanking her anytime soon.

"What if the killer had still been inside that apartment?" he demanded. "What if he'd come at you with that knife?"

She had mace in her bag. Not much as a weapon, but it was *something.* "No one was there when I arrived."

"You sure about that?"

Pretty sure since she'd gone through every room in that place. "I—"

"Gabrielle?" A surprised voice. Male. Rough. Very distinct.

When a woman heard a voice like that—so deep and hard and rumbling—she didn't forget it.

She fantasized about it. She enjoyed it.

She didn't forget.

"What's going on?" That voice continued, and then a warm, strong hand closed over her shoulder. "Is somebody hurt?"

She turned and faced the owner of that sexy voice—Cooper Marshall. Tall, gorgeous and with a smile that had made her heart skip a beat the first time she met him.

In other words—trouble.

"Someone's dead," Lane said before she could respond to Cooper. "And if Gabrielle doesn't learn to be more careful, she could wind up the same way."

Cooper's fingers tightened on her shoulder. "Dead?"

"You need to clear out of here," Lane said, speaking to her and giving another of his firm nods. Lane liked his firm nods. "There's no way any civilians are going to get near that crime scene tonight."

That was not what Gabrielle wanted to hear.

She had definite plans to explore that apartment, because she suspected that Lockwood had been in possession of some evidence that she could use.

"Catch the train, Gabby," Lane advised her as he turned away, "and call it a night."

A police car pulled away.

Cooper kept holding her. His touch sure felt warm.

She glanced at him again. Cooper was wearing black—a black T-shirt and pants, and the guy actually seemed to blend with the night. For such a big guy, she'd found that he blended easily.

But then again, he'd told her that he was a P.I. Private investigators were supposed to be extremely good at blending.

"What did you stumble on this time?" Cooper asked her, the growl kicking up in his words.

"Oh, the usual." She tried to keep the tremble from her voice. *Failed.* "A witness who was murdered before he could talk to me."

Cooper swore.

Yes, yes, that was how she felt, too.

"Forget the train. I'll take you home." Then he was pulling her with him and away from the crowd that had gathered on the street. "I was on my way home when I saw the lights. I thought I'd stop by and see what was happening." He spared her a glance. "A dead man, Gabrielle?"

Yes, well, finding Lockwood dead hadn't exactly been on her agenda.

Cooper's motorcycle waited at the side of the road. He climbed on then tossed her the helmet. "Just hold on tight, and I'll have you home soon."

She caught the helmet, but hesitated.

"What?" The light from the streetlamp fell on his face. It glinted off his dark blond hair and made him look even more handsome—and dangerous. "Don't you trust me for a little ride? Come on, we're neighbors. It's not like the trip is out of my way."

He was right. They were neighbors. They shared a brownstone—just the two of them.

When she'd moved in four months ago, she hadn't been sure what to expect from her male neighbor. Her landlord had told her that Cooper regularly worked out of the country, that she probably wouldn't hear a peep from him.

She'd heard some peeps. And so far, he hadn't been out of the country.

On her first day in the apartment, she'd baked him chocolate chip cookies. She had a thing about baking—it soothed her. So she'd strolled down with her cookies to say hello.

She'd gotten a good look at him, standing in the doorway, tall and sexy, and she'd almost dropped those cookies.

"Gabrielle?"

She shoved on her helmet and climbed onto the motorcycle behind Cooper.

He laughed. "You're going to have to sit a little closer than that. And put your arms around me."

She'd put her arms *behind* herself and was currently gripping the back of the seat.

He revved the engine. The bike kicked to life and when it shot forward, her hands flew up and wrapped around Cooper.

She gripped him as tightly as she could.

All muscle.

She could feel his rock-hard abs beneath her hands. No big surprise. She'd heard him working out before. Boxing. The guy loved to punch.

She'd seen him sporting an assortment of bruises since she'd met him, so she figured he must do more than just hit his punching bag. The guy probably fought at a local ring. The image of Cooper, bare-chested, fighting...well, that was an image that had sure floated in her mind before.

The motorcycle zoomed through the city, flying through intersections, cutting closely around corners. At one point, Gabrielle had to squeeze her eyes shut because she was pretty certain they were going to crash and become nothing but a mangled pile of limbs.

"We're here."

Her eyes cracked open. Sure enough, they'd made it to the brownstone. Located off the main streets and nestled in one of the few, quiet corners of D.C., the brownstone stood with its porch lights blazing.

She loved that place.

"You can…um, release that grip on me now," Cooper told her.

Gabrielle realized that her nails were digging into his shirt—into him. "Sorry," she muttered and jumped from the bike. "I'm not exactly a motorcycle fan."

He shoved down the kickstand, and then took his time rising from the bike. "Really? And here I thought you liked to live on the wild side."

What? Since when?

"Coming in at all hours of the night," he murmured as he brushed past her and headed up the steps that would take them inside the brownstone. "Covering the most dangerous cases in the city. You sure seem like a woman who enjoys living on the edge."

She wasn't going to touch that one.

As they paused on the narrow porch, the wind chime that she'd hung up a few days before pealed softly. The sound soothed her, at least a little bit.

Gabrielle followed him inside. A large, curving bannister led to the apartment upstairs. Her place was up there. His apartment was downstairs, right below hers. They both had a key to the main door, and she watched as he secured that door.

He'd gotten her home, so this was where they should part ways. Only she found herself hesitant to leave him. Maybe it was the image she still had of poor Keith Lockwood. *I can still smell the blood.* No, she wasn't in a hurry to rush up those stairs and spend the night all by herself.

Gabrielle already knew sleep wouldn't come easily. She'd be too busy remembering the sight of that body.

So she lingered at the foot of the stairs, studying Cooper.

He turned toward her and cocked his head. Then his eyes, a shade of a blue that electrified her, narrowed. "You're scared." He stalked toward her.

Gabrielle stiffened at the accusation. "I'm a little shaken. I found a dead body. I *get* to be shaken."

He stopped less than a foot from her. "I'm sorry you had to see that."

"Yes, well, I'm sorry that Mr. Lockwood is dead. Maybe if we'd met earlier, if I'd just gone by his place sooner instead of waiting for our meeting time—"

"Then you might be dead, too," he said, cutting through her words.

Gabrielle pushed back her hair. "He asked me to meet him. He called and said that he had a tip for me." *So much blood.* "I guess someone wanted to make sure he never got the chance to deliver that tip."

He took her hand.

Her breath rushed out. In four months, he hadn't touched her. Until tonight. He'd touched her at the crime scene, and now he was touching her here.

She hadn't expected his touch to unsettle her so much. But it did. Awareness pulsed through her as she stared into his eyes.

"Come with me," he invited softly. "You shouldn't be alone after what happened."

"I'm always alone."

He frowned.

Wait, those words had come out wrong. That was her problem. She was good at *writing.* When she was talking, Gabrielle had a tendency to say the wrong thing. She cleared her throat and tried again, "What I meant was that I don't mind being alone. It's late, and I should be getting upstairs."

He used his grip on her hand to tug her toward him. "It's late all right, but I'm betting you've got so much adrenaline pumping through your body that sleep is the last thing on your mind." His eyes glittered down at her. The guy easily topped six foot two, maybe six foot three, and he had the wide, broad shoulders that a football player would envy.

When she looked up at him then, she didn't see the danger that she normally perceived.

She saw strength. Safety.

"I know a thing or two about adrenaline rushes. I can help you ride it out."

He didn't mean that sexually, did he? Because they were nowhere close to having a sexual relationship. No matter what a few heated dreams might have told her.

"Come on." He guided her toward his door. She'd never actually been past the threshold of his place, so curiosity stirred within her.

Curiosity. It had been her downfall since she was a kid.

He opened the door. The alarm immediately began to beep, and he quickly punched in a code to reset the system.

"Why don't you have a seat on the couch?" Cooper offered. "I'll grab us both a drink."

Her gaze shifted around the room. Ah…there was the punching bag hanging from the ceiling in what looked like a workout room that branched from the living area.

The hardwood floor gleamed in the apartment. A leather couch and armchair were centered around a very large TV. Typical. What wasn't so typical…

She didn't see a single family photograph.

Actually, there were no photographs at all in the place.

The walls were bare and painted a light brown. A small hallway snaked off to the left, and she found herself leaning forward to peer down that dark corridor.

"My bedroom is back that way. The guest room, too." His breath blew against her ear and Gabrielle gave a little jump. She hadn't even heard him approach. "There something in particular you're hoping to see?" Cooper asked

"Ah, no, nothing." She pasted a fake smile on her face and turned toward him. "I don't know why I came in here. I should let you get some rest."

"I don't sleep much." He lifted his right hand. His tanned fingers had curved around a clear glass. "For you."

"Thanks." She put it to her lips and nearly choked when she took a gulp.

Whiskey.

"A few sips might help you to calm your nerves."

Uh, *no.*

He downed his own glass in seemingly one swallow. "It's been one hell of a night," he muttered as he set his glass down on the nearby end table.

She put her glass down, too. The whiskey was

burning her throat. When it came to drinking, she was way too much of a lightweight.

"You don't want to take the edge off?" Cooper asked her, frowning slightly.

She sank into the couch. *I should be heading for the door.* "I don't mix so well with whiskey."

"I can make you something else..."

"No." The leather was supple beneath her fingers. Tension still held her body tight, and she kept thinking—

"It doesn't do any good to keep picturing the dead." Cooper sat next to her. His thighs brushed against hers. "Turn around."

"Wh-what?" Now that was just sad. He was making her so nervous that she was actually stuttering.

"You're so stiff you're driving *me* crazy," he said.

She turned around. His hands reached for her shoulders. Oh, no, there was no way those fighting fists were going to give any kind of relaxing massage—

His fingers began to knead her flesh.

Gabrielle's eyes nearly rolled back in her head. She was wrong. So very wrong. His fingers were magic.

"I can help you to relax. Just breathe. Don't picture him. Get that image out of your head."

The man was way too good with his hands. "Is this…how you usually deal with adrenaline?"

A soft laugh. "No, I usually use sex."

The tension snapped right back in her shoulders.

"Relax," Cooper ordered, "that wasn't an offer."

Oh, right.

"Unless you want it to be…"

Trouble. She'd known that the guy was serious trouble from day one.

"What cold case are you working on?" He asked before she could do more than suck in a shocked gasp of air. "I know you told me that you were starting to profile them."

She had told him that, during one of their brief two-minute conversations when their paths occasionally crossed. "Kylie Archer. Her case isn't as old as the others, but the cops don't have any leads, so I thought I could try digging."

"That digging led you to the body?"

"Keith Lockwood," she whispered. The image of his body tried to push into her mind again, but she shoved it back.

He kept rubbing her shoulders. His broad fingers were sliding down her back.

Her thighs shifted restlessly.

"He knew who killed the woman?"

"I don't know." She would find out. As soon as

the cops backed off, Gabrielle would be making her way back inside that apartment.

Her eyes drifted closed as he kept caressing her skin. His fingers skimmed over the edge of her arms. Then he returned his attention to her shoulders, started working down. Down…

He pushed lightly against her lower back.

Gabrielle had to bite back a moan. That felt so *good.*

But…was a massage supposed to turn a girl on?

*This one is. No, correction...*he *is.*

"You didn't see any sign of anyone else in that place?"

"The door was open when I went inside. Someone had shattered the lock. When I saw that, I knew something was wrong."

His fingers stilled. "You knew something was wrong, and you *still* went rushing in? You should have called the cops first!"

"Lockwood could've been hurt. That's why I went in. As soon as I saw the body, I called 911."

"Next time," his deep voice rumbled as he started his massage once more, "do me a favor, okay? Call the cops before you rush in and find yourself facing a killer."

She wanted to melt into a puddle. His hands were heaven. The tension was gone. Well, all but the sexual tension. The sensual awareness she felt was heating up.

And that's my sign to leave.

His fingers were very close to her hips. And she was arching against his touch like a cat.

Get a grip, Gabrielle. It's just a massage. It's not lovemaking.

But she almost wished that it was.

Gabrielle jerked away from his touch. "I have to go." She jumped to her feet.

He stared up at her.

"Thanks for the ride home. And the drink. And the massage." She was rambling. "Good night." Then she scrambled for the door.

"Gabrielle."

His voice stopped her just as her fingers closed around the doorknob.

"If you get scared, if you need someone to talk to, I'm here."

Good to know. She tossed him a quick, nervous smile, then she fled. No other word for it.

A smart woman ran from trouble.

THE WOMAN WAS going to be trouble.

He'd known that, of course, the minute she moved in.

Long, black hair, golden skin, dark eyes… And a body that sure made him want to sin.

Gabrielle Harper was the last person he'd expected to find in his life. A reporter, right upstairs?

Fate had a twisted sense of humor.

If Gabrielle ever found out what he really did for a living, if she found out about the secret government group known as the EOD—

Can't happen.

There were only a few civilians with clearance to possess intel about the Elite Operations Division. Too-pretty and too-tempting Gabrielle couldn't learn about his group.

Secrecy meant survival for the EOD agents. He would do anything to secure that survival.

Anything necessary. Those were his orders, after all. They'd come straight down from the top—from the director of the EOD, Bruce Mercer.

And anything necessary…well, that included a little breaking and entering.

Cooper had waited a few hours, until he was sure that Gabrielle had finally drifted into slumber. Then he'd commenced his B&E routine.

It was ridiculously easy to get inside Gabrielle's place. Since *he'd* installed the locks right before she moved in, Cooper had a key to her apartment.

He also knew her security code.

Again, because *he'd* installed the system.

She'd left a light on in her hallway. The faint glow spilled into the living area.

Her place was an exact copy of his. Only instead of a workout area, Gabrielle had an office in that side space.

The office was his destination. But first, he had to make sure that he wouldn't be disturbed.

He crept toward her bedroom. Cooper pushed the door open just a few inches.

Another light was on in there. A closet light this time.

Gabrielle didn't like the darkness. Odd, considering that her job sent her right into the dark path of criminals every day.

The glow fell on the bed, on her.

She'd kicked away her covers, and she lay on her side. Gabrielle wore a pair of jogging shorts and a faded college T-shirt. Her legs were long and bare and perfect.

Killer legs. Truly killer.

Her eyes were closed. Her right hand curled, palm up, on the edge of the bed. Sexy and vulnerable—a dangerous combination.

He took a deep breath and smelled her. A light scent. Lilac. He knew it only because she *always* smelled that way. He'd had to figure out the scent because it was driving him crazy.

The first day he'd met her, she'd come to him, a sweet smile on her face and a tray of chocolate chip cookies in her hands.

He'd gobbled up the cookies. He'd wanted to gobble *her* up. He still did.

Focus on the job.

Carefully, Cooper backed away from the door.

Then he made his way to the office. Booting up her computer was easy. Figuring out her password was a bit harder. Luckily, he'd had some help from the EOD on that end.

Another agent, Sydney Sloan Ortez, had created a program that let him bypass most security walls on systems like Gabrielle's.

It took sixty seconds, and he was in.

He found Gabrielle's files on Lockwood. With a few clicks, he transferred copies of those files to his flash drive.

Then… *Sorry, sweetheart, I hate to do it but…* He uploaded a virus to her computer.

The EOD didn't want Gabrielle getting involved in Lockwood's murder. Mercer had given him an order to throw her off the killer's scent.

Now they had her case notes. Her files.

She'd have to start over from scratch once again. That would buy him some time.

Enough time to hunt a killer.

WELL, WELL, WELL…

It seemed that Cooper Marshall was the agent on his trail.

He'd seen Cooper in the crowd outside of Lockwood's place. He'd known the reporter was going to meet Keith, so figuring out that the police would be called after midnight hadn't been exactly hard.

He'd watched the scene with interest.

He certainly hadn't expected to see Cooper Marshall rush through the crowd and go straight to the reporter's side.

Then to *leave* with the woman…

Interesting.

Perhaps Gabrielle Harper was more important than he'd originally thought.

He would learn more about her. Then he would determine…was she valuable enough to bring into his game?

Or was she a pawn that could be eliminated?

Chapter Two

Gabrielle slid under the yellow police tape that blocked the entrance to Keith Lockwood's apartment. The cops had tried to repair the lock on his door, but their attempt hadn't been exactly successful.

That lack of success made getting in much easier for her.

She'd waited for night to fall once more. Waited to make sure all the cops had cleared out of the place.

She wasn't waiting any longer.

Gabrielle tiptoed into the apartment. She didn't turn on any lights. Lights would be seen from the street below, and she wasn't about to advertise her B&E stint.

So instead of turning on the overhead lights, Gabrielle pulled out a small flashlight. She crept carefully through the apartment. Her first stop was the desk near the kitchen. She opened the top drawer.

Empty.

The second drawer—

Empty.

The third—

Totally cleaned out.

Her eyes narrowed. There had been a computer on that desk last night. It was gone now, so she'd have to check in with Lane to see if the cops had confiscated it. No doubt, they had. Their tech department would search it and when they were finished, she'd just call in a favor from said tech department and get them to spill their results to her.

She turned away from the desk. There were other places to search.

Like the room where she'd found the body.

Her shoulders squared as she headed down the hallway. The scent of death still hung in the air. She hated that smell.

Her foot pressed down on the wooden floor. The long, low creak made her stiffen, but she kept going.

Then she was in the bedroom. Her flashlight illuminated the floor and the outline of the body. The blood had stained the wood.

So much blood.

Gabrielle exhaled. She hoped that Lockwood had died quickly. No one deserved to suffer.

She forced herself to look away from that

outline. Her gaze and her light darted around the room. She could see a chest of drawers, a dresser and a nightstand. No photographs. *Just like Cooper's place.*

That wasn't normal. She edged closer to the nightstand positioned to the right of the bed. People usually kept photographs of family and friends in their homes. Light touches to personalize the place.

At the edge of the bed, her foot stepped down on something hard.

She heard the crunch of glass.

Gabrielle winced—*so much for being good at crime scenes*—and she bent down. She'd stepped on a frame. One that had dropped to the floor and slipped under the edge of the bed.

So Lockwood did have at least one picture.

She turned the frame over. Pieces of broken glass fell onto the bed.

Her light scanned over that photo. Her breath came faster. Her heart raced.

The picture was of Keith Lockwood. He was smiling in the picture, and he had his arm around a pretty, blonde woman.

Gabrielle easily recognized Kylie Archer. She'd seen plenty of pictures of that woman before.

What were you going to tell me about her? What? Gabrielle sure wished the dead could talk.

She backed away from the bed, still studying the photo. Backed away and backed *into* someone.

Someone big and strong.

Gabrielle opened her mouth to scream.

The scream never escaped because a hard hand covered her mouth. And even as that hand covered her mouth, an arm rose around Gabrielle and jerked her closer to—

"Easy," that familiar deep voice told her, as Cooper's breath blew against the shell of her ear. "I'm not going to hurt you, and a scream would just send the neighbors rushing to call the police."

Because he'd scared her, Gabrielle elbowed him in the ribs. He let her go with a grunt.

Gabrielle whirled to confront him. "What are you doing here? This is a crime scene!" She aimed her light right at his face.

He winced. "Trying to blind me?"

She thought that might only be fair since he'd just tried to scare her to death.

"And, yes, I know it's a crime scene," he said, sounding aggrieved. "That's why I wondered what the hell you were doing in here."

"You followed me?" Her voice was a whisper. He must have followed her. There was no other explanation. But why?

He shrugged. "After last night, maybe I was a little worried about you."

Oh. Wait. That was…nice.

The sneaking up on her part? *Not so nice.* "I didn't even hear you." Not so much as a sound.

"I'm used to sneaking in and out of places."

His comment sounded a bit sinister.

"And speaking of *out,* we need to go." But he was frowning now. "What are you holding?"

Her right hand gripped the flashlight. Her left still held the picture frame.

She took the light off his face and let it fall on the photo. "See how close they are? The way his hand is wrapped around her? I think Lockwood and Kylie Archer were involved." Lovers. Their bodies rested so easily against each other. "And, judging by the way they were killed—with their throats slit and with no sign of defensive wounds on their bodies—I'm also suspecting that the same person killed them both."

Silence.

She'd expected more after her big reveal. Gabrielle cleared her throat.

"How do you know there were no defensive wounds?" Cooper asked.

"Because I had time to check Lockwood's body before the cops got here." She also knew exactly what to look for regarding those types of wounds. "The thing that doesn't fit for me is the broken lock. Kylie's home didn't have a broken lock. Her door was locked, from the inside, and the cops were the ones to break their way inside."

Again…more silence. She wasn't really used to working with someone else on her stories, but she expected him to say something.

"Uh, Cooper?"

"Leave the picture. We need to go *now.*"

"But I want to search some more. I need to—"

"When I parked, I saw a cop car coming down the street. I double-timed it up here to you, because I was worried the officer might be coming in for a sweep."

Her eyes widened. She dropped the photo to the floor. Mostly in the same spot. "We need to go *now.*"

She grabbed his hand and rushed down the hallway.

She dodged the squeaky floorboard.

So did he.

She paused. He hadn't stepped on the squeaky floorboard when he'd first come in the apartment, either. The squeak would have alerted her to his presence. "How did you—"

"Hurry."

She kept going. She slid under the police tape, hustled into the hallway.

And heard footsteps.

Gabrielle darted to the edge of the stairs, and she saw the cop. Lucky for her, he was looking down, not up, so he didn't see her.

Cooper wrapped his arm around her waist

and hauled her back. "Come on." He pulled her with him.

Lockwood's apartment was the only one on that floor. There weren't exactly a ton of places for them to hide.

"Storage," he muttered, moving toward a narrow, white door.

She hadn't even *seen* that door at first.

He opened it and pushed her inside.

It was the size of a closet. A very small, very overstuffed closet. Her body plastered against his.

"Not a sound," Cooper barely breathed the words.

She gave a jerky nod. Gabrielle could hear the footsteps then. The cop going to the apartment, going right past the storage closet.

But what if he comes back?

The closet smelled of ammonia. It had to be where the cleaning supplies were kept for the building. It was pitch-dark in there, so she couldn't see anything, and Gabrielle wasn't about to turn on her light.

There was silence in the hallway.

She figured the silence meant that the cop had entered the apartment.

If Cooper hadn't gotten me out of there, the cop would have walked right in on me.

Explaining her way out of that situation wouldn't have been easy.

Cooper still had his arm around her. Her hips and derriere pressed against him. Her back was to his chest. She could feel the steady rhythm of his breaths.

He didn't seem shaken. Not even a little.

Meanwhile her own breath seemed to heave out far too loudly.

She didn't move, didn't try to ease away from Cooper. She was too afraid she'd stumble onto another piece of flooring that would creak and give away their position.

After a seeming eternity, the cop's footsteps sounded in the hallway again.

The footsteps faded away as he descended the stairs.

Her shoulders slumped. She tried to pull away from Cooper.

"Not yet. Let's give him a chance to get good and gone."

She stilled. Tight, dark spaces weren't so high up on her list of favorite things. Actually, they were dead last on that list. But she wasn't alone right then. That was something.

Cooper. Why did she feel so safe with him? A man she barely knew?

Because he just saved you and you're going to owe him now.

"Can you try..." He whispered in her ear. She shivered as he continued, "Can you try to avoid committing any more crimes for the next few days?"

"No promises," she whispered back. "My computer crashed, and I'm back to square one on this case." Not totally true. She had backup files.

Not an amateur.

His hold eased. "I think we've waited long enough. Let's just head out, nice and slow, okay? Follow my lead."

Right. She could do that.

He opened the door, looked to the left and the right. He went down the stairs first. Cooper kept a tight hold on her hand when they escaped from that building.

Then they were outside. The night air was muggy and thick, and it felt like heaven after the ammonia-filled confines of that closet.

"Thanks," she began with a weary smile, "I needed your—"

His eyes had been over her shoulder, on the street, but he suddenly grabbed her and yanked her close.

Cooper kissed her.

It wasn't some easy, getting-to-know-you kiss. Not tentative. Not light.

It was hot. Hard. Openmouthed.

Toe-curling.

Fantastic.

His arms wrapped around her. He lifted her up

against him, and Gabrielle's toes barely skimmed the ground.

His tongue licked across her bottom lip then thrust into her mouth. He tasted her. He claimed. He—

"The cop was still here," Cooper growled against her lips. "I didn't want him suspicious."

He was kissing her for a cover.

Had she moaned? She'd definitely sunk her nails into his shoulders. She'd even arched against him.

"I—I know," she lied. Their mouths were barely an inch apart. "The kiss was a good idea."

A car cranked. The engine growled.

"I'm guessing that's him," Gabrielle said as she kept her hands on Cooper. But she did retract her nails. "Pulling away?"

He nodded. "I'm not letting you go until he's gone."

His body was so warm.

The kiss had been a fake.

Humiliating. Maybe she'd played it off, though. Maybe.

They stood there, embracing, mouths so incredibly close, and in that moment, Gabrielle realized a very important fact.

Cooper was aroused.

If she hadn't been so distracted a moment before, she would have been keyed in to that situation sooner. She was so focused on the hot feel of his mouth she hadn't realized until now that the hips thrusting against her—

He freed her.

Gabrielle stopped feeling quite so humiliated. He had been affected by the kiss. Mr. Dangerous had gotten just as caught up as she had in the heat of the moment.

"We need to get home," he said in that deep rumble of his. "Come on, my bike's waiting."

Her phone vibrated, jerking in her pocket. She'd turned the ringer off before her little stint of B&E. "Hold on," Gabrielle told him. She yanked out her phone and recognized her boss's number at the *Inquisitor*.

"Gabrielle..." Cooper gritted out.

"It's my boss. Calling after midnight. I have to take this." Because there was only one reason Hugh Peters would call her this late.

A story.

"What is it, Hugh?"

"I just heard on the police scanner..." Excitement thickened his voice. "They got another vic. A female. Same MO as Archer."

Her fingers tightened around the phone. "Where."

He rattled off the address.

The address was close, just a few blocks away. She could jog there.

She *would* jog there.

"You get there and you find out what the hell is happening, got it?" Hugh said. Before she could answer, he continued, "Three kills? This mess is starting to look like the work of a serial."

His words chilled her. "We can't know that, not yet."

Cooper's gaze was on her.

"Get there and find out," Hugh ordered.

She shoved the phone back into her pocket. "Thanks for the offer of the ride, but my night's not over yet."

No wonder the cop had rushed away. She tilted her head and heard the wail of sirens in the distance.

Cooper stiffened. "What's happened?"

"Another woman has been found with her throat cut." She spun away from him. It was a good thing she jogged regularly. "I'll see you later, Cooper. Thanks for the help!"

He grabbed her wrist. "You're racing to a murder scene?"

"It's what I do." He was slowing her down.

Cooper shook his head. "Going on foot isn't the way. I can get you there faster." He pointed to his waiting motorcycle. "Just give me the address, and I'm there."

She didn't want to waste time arguing. She

called out the address even as she climbed onto the bike. Seconds later they were racing away.

"IT LOOKS LIKE the same MO," Cooper said into his phone. He'd backed away from the crowd, found the best cover of shadows, and now he watched the chaotic scene with a careful gaze. "One of the cops said that the victim was a woman named Melanie Farrell."

"She's not one of ours," the clipped voice on the other end of the line responded. That voice belonged to Bruce Mercer. Cooper's boss. A man who knew where every single secret was buried in D.C.

Mostly because his job was to bury those secrets.

"You sure about that?" Cooper pressed. "She was found in her apartment, with the doors locked. Her throat was slit, and there were no signs of a struggle."

A low whistle. "You sure learned a lot on this one, fast."

His gaze tracked over to Gabrielle. She was currently talking quickly to a uniformed cop. The cop looked nervous. Since Gabrielle was grilling him, the guy should be nervous. "I had a little help." She'd been the one to get all of those details.

"The reporter." A long sigh slipped from Mercer. "I thought you had her contained."

Containing Gabrielle was a bit of a challenge. It was a good thing that he liked challenges. "I can use her. The cops tell her more in a few minutes than they would ever reveal to me." He had the P.I. cover for a reason, but Gabrielle's resources were proving to be far more useful.

Gabrielle eased away from the cop and gazed up at the building.

Trying to find a way inside, aren't you?

She edged toward the left, moving near the alley that he knew snaked behind those apartments.

"Melanie Farrell is *not* one of our agents." Mercer was adamant. "She shouldn't be targeted by our rogue."

The rogue—the EOD agent that Cooper was hunting.

"Kylie Archer wasn't an agent, either," Cooper said, going with his gut.

"Who?"

"She was killed a few months ago. Again, same damn MO."

"Our guy has been busy." Anger heated Mercer's words.

Our guy. Because they did think it was one of their own. One who'd tried to attack Mercer by going after his daughter and now…

"I found out that Kylie was romantically involved with Keith." Well, Gabrielle had found that out.

He couldn't see her now. Cooper's body tensed.

"The guy tried to get at you by taking away the one person who mattered," Cooper said.

Mercer's daughter.

"He couldn't get her, so maybe he decided to attack other agents by going after the people they valued." It was a theory that he was just developing, but so far, the pieces fit.

"That idea only plays," Mercer said slowly, "if we can link Melanie to an EOD agent."

"Sydney can find a link." If anyone could, it would be here. Sydney Sloan Ortez was in charge of information retrieval for the EOD. When it came to computers, no one was better. She could dig into any person's life with her machines. Could, and had.

"I'll get her started," Mercer promised. "In the meantime, you keep tracking this rogue. He knows our agents, he knows us, but I'll be damned if he's going to get away with these attacks on my watch."

Mercer hung up. Cooper pushed the phone into his back pocket. Gabrielle had slipped into the alley, and she'd never glanced back to see if anyone was watching her.

She should learn to pay attention to what—*who*—was behind her.

He'd sure gotten the drop on her easily enough in that apartment. If he *had* been the killer, she would have died.

His back teeth ground together as he stalked toward the alley. He'd had no idea that his neighbor was so drawn to danger.

Just like me. But he knew why he liked the thrill that came from danger. That burst of adrenaline made him feel alive.

What drew Gabrielle into the darkness?

THE FIRE ESCAPE led all the way up the side of the building. Gabrielle studied that fire escape, considering the options. It would sure be easy enough for the killer to slide through a window in the victim's apartment then flee down the fire escape.

Was that why the front door was locked? Did you get out this way?

She slipped deeper into the alley. The voices were muted here. Her shoe brushed over a discarded aluminum can. The acrid odor of rotten garbage was strong in that alley.

Gabrielle glanced to the left. A green garbage container sat to the side. The alley snaked away a bit then opened to another street.

Since there were no lights in that area, it would have been easy enough for the killer to hide down there.

"You're in the wrong place."

The whisper drifted to her. When the words sank in, Gabrielle froze.

"You shouldn't be here, all alone..."

She whirled around. That voice was coming from the shadows near the garbage container. "Who's there? Show yourself!"

Laughter. Low and chilling. "Not yet…not yet…"

Goose bumps rose on her arms.

"Gabrielle!"

That was Cooper. A shout had never sounded more wonderful.

Before she could call out to him, something—someone—grabbed her and shoved her into the brick wall of the alley. Her head hit the bricks, hard, and her body slumped.

"Not yet..." That whisper told her once more.

Then she didn't hear anything else.

SHE HADN'T ANSWERED HIM.

Cooper rushed forward, running fast. She'd just been out of his sight for a few minutes. The cops were close by. Gabrielle couldn't just vanish.

A crumpled form lay curled near a garbage container.

Gabrielle.

He didn't realize that he'd bellowed her name. But in the next instant, he was on his knees beside her, frantically searching for a pulse at the base of her throat.

The pulse beat slow, steady, beneath his fingers.

He brushed back her hair. Her head slumped weakly against his hold.

What in the hell had happened?

His gaze flew around the alley. It was too dark to see much.

And he didn't hear anyone.

"Gabrielle?" His fingers shifted through her hair. When he found the bump on the side of her head, he swore.

Then he stood, holding her carefully in his arms. She needed help.

"Freeze!" a male's voice shouted.

He wasn't in the mood to freeze. He was in the mood to get Gabrielle help.

Light from a flashlight hit him in the face. That light was so blinding that it made viewing the person connected to that voice hard. The man was little more than a shadow.

"Gabrielle?" The guy's voice roughened. "What the hell did you do to her?"

"Nothing," Cooper growled. "When I found her, she was unconscious. I'm trying to help her." *And you're slowing me down.*

The light came closer.

"I'm not armed," Cooper told him. That wasn't true, but the man wouldn't notice the weapons he carried. They were too well concealed. "We need to get her help."

He could see the man's face now. It was the detective from the other night, Lane Carmichael.

"I remember you," Carmichael said, obviously placing him. "You were at the other crime scene, too."

Great. *Not* the connection Cooper wanted the detective to make. If he wasn't careful, the cops would start looking at him for the kills.

He wasn't sure his P.I. cover could stand up to their perusal.

Carmichael yanked out his radio and called for backup—and an EMT.

A moan slipped from Gabrielle's lips. Under the flashlight, her lashes began to flutter. She blinked a few times then seemed to focus on him. "C-Cooper?"

"It's all right," he tried to reassure her. "I've got you."

A faint smile curved her lips. "S-saving me... again? You're making a h-habit of it..."

Yes, he was.

The EMT ran toward him. The man reached for Gabrielle.

For an instant, Cooper had the crazy urge to keep holding her. *I don't want to let her go.*

But he never got too close to anyone or anything. That was the way he wanted his life to be. The way it had always been.

He let her go.

As she was taken away from him, Cooper's shoulders tensed. He was going to find out exactly what had happened to Gabrielle in that alley.

Once more, his gaze swept the area, but he didn't see anything out of the ordinary.

With this killer, I wouldn't.

The ambulance's siren blared, and Cooper found himself hurrying toward that sound.

HE HADN'T BEEN able to resist. The woman had been right there. All alone.

She was the one who kept digging into his life.

So he'd thought it would only be fair that he started to play with *her* life.

The fact that she was connected to Cooper Marshall was just bonus. The connection made things even more interesting.

I can use her.

But not yet. She didn't matter enough. Not yet.

He whistled as he walked down the street. Plenty of tourists were still out. Even this late, the streets were full of people.

It was easy to blend with those people. To walk right past the overworked cops.

Cooper had climbed into the ambulance. He

was playing hero. That wasn't a role well suited to the man.

He and Cooper were a lot alike. That was why Mercer had Cooper hunting him.

Darkness clung to them both. They were loners. Killers.

In the end, though, only one of them would survive this game.

It wouldn't be Cooper.

Pity. He'd once called the man friend.

Now, he just thought of Cooper Marshall as a target.

Chapter Three

Gabrielle took a deep breath. She squared her shoulders, smoothed her skirt. Then she lifted her hand and knocked soundly on Cooper's door.

She had a proposition for him, one that she very much hoped he'd accept. She wanted—

The door swung open. Only Cooper wasn't the person standing on the other side of that door.

A very pretty woman with glass-sharp cheekbones and shoulder-length black hair stared back at Gabrielle.

A date. He's on a date. The kiss—the one she ridiculously thought about far too much—had been fake. As good-looking as Cooper was, *of course,* the guy had a pretty girlfriend.

"Can I help you with something?" The woman asked. Her voice was smooth. Friendly. Her smile was a little uncertain.

"I was looking for Cooper."

"He's in the shower—"

The floor could truly open up and swallow

her. She'd been indulging in some serious fantasy time with Cooper, and he'd been…busy… with this lady.

"—but you're welcome to come in and wait for him, if you'd like." The woman backed up, pulling the door open a few more inches. "You're his neighbor, right? The reporter?"

She didn't want to cross that threshold. She didn't want to, but Gabrielle still needed Cooper's help. "Yes. I am." She offered her hand. "Gabrielle Harper."

The woman's shake was firm and warm. "I'm Rachel."

You weren't supposed to dislike people you didn't know. She'd just met pretty Rachel. Rachel seemed friendly. Rachel also seemed to be eyeing her with a gaze that was a little too assessing.

Then Cooper appeared. He strode down the hallway, a pair of jeans hanging low on his hips. No shirt. His hair was wet. *Fresh from the shower.*

When he saw Gabrielle, he came to a very fast and hard stop.

"Company," Rachel murmured as she dropped Gabrielle's hand. A faint smile curled her lips. "I was just getting acquainted with your nice neighbor."

Cooper's blue gaze narrowed. Then he started walking again, a determined stride that carried him right to Gabrielle. "How's your head?" His hands lifted, as if he'd touch her head. "I'm sorry I left you at the hospital—I'm not family, so the doctors wouldn't let me stay with you."

She caught his hands, flushed. "I'm fine. My dad always did say that I had a hard head."

He didn't smile. "You were unconscious in that alley. When I first saw you, I was afraid that you were dead."

She was still holding his hands in front of his girlfriend. This scene was so awkward. She stepped back. "I didn't mean to interrupt when you had company. I can come back later." She sidled toward the door. "It was, uh, nice to meet you, Rachel." *Total lie.*

Cooper gave a rough bark of laughter. "Rachel isn't company. She's—" But then he broke off, frowning. "Wait, who do you think she is?"

That was a weird question, but Gabrielle blurted, "Girlfriend?"

Rachel was the one to laugh then. "He should be so lucky." She bent and scooped up a designer bag. "We're just friends. No worries on that score." She winked at Gabrielle. "Maybe that makes it nicer to meet me?"

It did.

Rachel inclined her head toward Cooper. "And maybe you can meet up with me and Dylan later? I know he'd love to get an update on you."

Cooper gave a quick nod. "Will do."

It had to be her imagination, but Gabrielle could have sworn the enthusiasm in his voice was faked.

Rachel slipped away a few moments later, and Cooper locked the door behind her.

Gabrielle's hands twisted in front of her. It had been almost two days since she'd last seen him. She'd thought about him plenty during that time.

Especially when the flowers arrived at the hospital—lilacs, her favorite. There hadn't been a card, just the flowers.

"You sure that you're okay?" He took her elbow and guided her to the couch.

She'd be better—less distracted—if he put on a shirt, but Gabrielle nodded. "I needed to thank you, both for finding me in that alley and for the flowers. I, um, lilacs are my favorite." She wore a lilac-scented body lotion, because she loved the smell so much.

His blond brows lifted. "How do you know they were from me?"

She blinked. Embarrassment burned through her. Since she wasn't dating anyone, she'd just assumed they were from him. "I—"

He laughed. "You sure are pretty when you blush. And, yes, they were from me." His fingers brushed back a lock of her hair. "I'm glad you liked them."

She had those lilacs upstairs, sitting in a vase

on her kitchen table. Every time she looked at them, she smiled.

But you're here on business. Don't get distracted. Gabrielle cleared her throat. "I need to ask you a few questions."

His hand lowered. She was hyperconscious of the strength of his body next to hers. "Sure. Give me just a minute, okay?" He rose and disappeared down the hallway.

She didn't move. She wanted to move. She wanted to pry and search—

Hold that curiosity back.

She stayed locked to the couch. He returned quickly, pulling a black T-shirt over his head. The man certainly seemed to enjoy wearing black.

"I was about to make some dinner. Want something?"

Gabrielle shook her head.

A half smile lifted his lips. "Come on, I make a mean spaghetti. It's a recipe I stole from Rachel. Her family's Italian, and *no one* does spaghetti better."

Her stomach growled.

"I'll take that as a yes," he murmured.

Then he headed into the kitchen. She heard pots and pans clanking. Gabrielle rose and followed after him. "I didn't come here so that you would fix me dinner."

He already had the water set to boil. Tomatoes were spread out on the counter.

"That's right," he said easily. "You came here to ask me questions. So ask."

While he cooked? She'd expected something a little more…businesslike.

"Ask." He sliced the tomatoes. Fast and with almost fanatical skill. She'd never seen anyone be so good with a knife.

"I…um…" She exhaled slowly. *Stop being frazzled with him.* "Did you see anyone else in that alley with me?"

He stopped slicing. He glanced at her, held her gaze. "It was dark. I could only see you."

That didn't mean that no one else had been there. "Did you hear anything?" Gabrielle asked carefully.

He dropped the pasta then came toward her while the sauce simmered. "No, I didn't hear anything." He propped against the counter and studied her. "Why?"

"Because I don't remember falling."

"After a head injury like yours, I know it's common to forget—"

"What I do remember," she said, speaking quickly and cutting through his words, "is a man's voice."

"What?"

"I told Lane—Detective Carmichael, but he

said the alley was searched thoroughly, both before and after my 'accident,' and there was no sign of anyone else there. Anyone else other than you, anyway."

Lane wasn't exactly a fan of Cooper's. In fact, he seemed pretty suspicious of Cooper. But then, Lane was suspicious of most folks. That was his nature.

"If you're trying to ask me if I slipped into the alley and slammed your head against a wall…" She saw Cooper's knuckles whiten as he clenched the edge of the countertop. "The answer is *no,* I didn't do that."

Gabrielle quickly shook her head. "That wasn't the question I was asking. I know you didn't do it. You're the guy who keeps rushing in to save me, not hurt me."

He blinked. A furrow appeared between his brows. "That's a whole lot of trust to give someone. You don't know me that well."

"I know you well enough to realize you aren't a killer."

He gazed steadily back at her. "Do you?"

What kind of response was that? It almost sounded as if he were trying to scare her. "Look, it wasn't your voice."

Cooper held up a hand. "You've lost me."

"I remember hearing a man's voice. It wasn't your voice."

Now there was doubt in his blue eyes. Lane had looked at her with the same doubt when she'd tried to explain this situation to him.

His hand fell back to his side. "There was a lot going on that night. It would be easy to get confused. Especially with that bump on your head."

"A minor concussion." She waved it away.

He stepped from the counter and caught her hand. "You don't shrug away an injury like that. Head injuries can be dangerous."

When he touched her, her heart beat faster. An electric current seemed to run through her body. *Just from a touch.* "That's why I stayed in the hospital. To make sure everything was okay." And because her boss at the paper had insisted on it. Hugh had told her she either stayed or she looked for a new job.

He didn't take kindly to his reporters being hurt.

She didn't take kindly to *being* hurt. "I know what I heard."

His gaze turned guarded. "Then tell me."

"A man grabbed me in that alley. He told me that I was in the wrong place." The memory of that rasping voice rolled through her mind. "And then he said...*not yet.*"

A muscle flexed in his jaw. "You don't remember his face?"

"I remember the feel of his hands grabbing me.

I remember the rasp of his voice, but his face?"

If only. "No, I don't remember that. I'm not even sure if I saw him. I was hoping that maybe you'd seen something."

"You were the only thing I saw."

He turned away from her. Cooper spent a few moments in silence as he finished preparing their meal.

"It could've been a mugger," she said to his back, as he reached for some plates. "I didn't have a purse with me, so maybe that's why he ran after I passed out."

"It could have been." He shut the cabinets with a rough motion of his hands.

"It could also have been the killer." That was her fear. Her suspicion. "I think he escaped the apartment by climbing down the fire escape. He fled through that alley. Maybe he dropped something. Maybe he had to go back for it." She followed him to the table. "Or maybe he was just one of those guys who enjoys going back to the scene of the crime. Someone who likes to watch the cops spin their wheels and come up with nothing."

He pulled out a chair for her. "Is that what the cops have?"

She eased into the seat. "Lane says there aren't any suspects. No prints, DNA or any other evidence was left at the scenes."

He sat across from her. He picked up his fork.

"I went back to all the crime scenes—" Gabrielle began.

The fork clattered against his plate.

"I didn't break in," she rushed to clarify, realizing how he must have interpreted her words. "I looked behind the buildings. Kylie Archer's place had a fire escape, too. The killer could easily have escaped on it."

"Lockwood didn't have a fire escape."

"No, he didn't." The spaghetti smelled fabulous. "But then again, maybe that's the reason why Lockwood's front door was smashed in. The attacker didn't have any other way to get inside, so he had to use force there."

Cooper ate in silence.

She took a bite of the spaghetti. He hadn't been lying. It was fantastic. "I'll have to make you one of my cherry pies," she said, sending him a nervous smile. "You did dinner, so I can do dessert."

His head tilted. His eyes heated, the blue getting even brighter. "Sounds like a date."

"I—" She nearly choked on the spaghetti. "I have a proposition for you."

That half smile flashed again. Did he have a dimple in his cheek? It looked like he did.

Sexy.

"I'd love to hear the proposition."

He made it sound…hot. It wasn't. She put her

fork down. "I want us to work together." She tried not to let the words come out as desperate.

He kept eating.

"I think we could make a good team. We could keep investigating the cases and find the killer—"

"I'm not in the market for a partner."

Okay. He was going to make her lay everything out for him. She'd have to show that desperation, after all. "But I am in the market for some protection." Because she was afraid, and Gabrielle didn't want to let the fear stop her from doing her job. "I think someone has been watching me. I think *he* has been watching me."

"TELL ME AGAIN..." Dylan Foxx began as he narrowed his eyes on Rachel Mancini. "Why is Cooper having a cozy dinner with the reporter? He's supposed to be keeping her out of this mess and not—"

"—seducing her?" Rachel finished. She'd seen the way Cooper looked at the other woman. She knew exactly what was on his mind.

Dylan shut the door of his office. They were in the EOD headquarters, a place most civilians would never visit. Actually, most civilians would never even know of its existence.

The EOD was a hybrid organization, one composed of former members of various military branches. The EOD had been founded and was still led by Bruce Mercer. The EOD was far off the books, and the agents took jobs that no one else could handle.

Jobs that often ended in violence. Death.

The EOD agents were the ones who went out after the hostages that *couldn't* be rescued. They were the ones who eliminated the most dangerous threats in the world.

Right now, unfortunately, one of those threats came from within.

A rogue agent.

Suspicion was rampant in the EOD. Trust, the cornerstone of the agency's success, was being shattered. If you couldn't trust the agent who had your back in the field, how were you supposed to complete the mission?

Rachel sank into the chair near Dylan's desk. She trusted him 100 percent. But she wasn't ready to extend that trust to all of the agents at the EOD.

They all knew how to kill, lie and keep secrets.

Someone was using those deadly skills.

"I could see them through the window," Rachel murmured. Not that she enjoyed the Peeping-Tom bit. "They went into the kitchen and the guy cooked."

"Cooper?" Dylan's dark brows shot up.

She nodded. "Maybe he's just trying to get under her guard. The lady has proven to be pretty resourceful."

"The lady's dangerous." He threw himself into the chair near her. Leather groaned. "I ran down her bio. She's got a trail of awards behind her and a reputation for being a real bulldog when it comes to her stories. She's latched on to our killer, and I don't see her just backing away now."

Not even after a trip to the hospital.

"The more time she spends with Cooper, the more likely she is to discover that his cover is a lie." Dylan ran a hand through his black hair. "The last thing we need is her trying to air a story on the EOD."

"We aren't on her radar." Rachel had done her own research on Gabrielle Harper. "She works to help victims. She's not even thinking about us."

"Not yet, she isn't. But if she's used to uncovering secrets, how long do you think it will be before she senses Cooper is hiding something from her?"

"Well that depends," Rachel said as her gaze held his, "on just how good Cooper is at lying. It's been my experience that some men are extremely talented when it comes to deceit."

There was a sharp rap at the door.

Dylan held her gaze for a moment longer. "You *know* you can trust me."

Yes, she did, as a partner, as a friend.

As a lover?

No, she couldn't risk that. She'd gone down the wrong path with a lover before. She still had the scars to prove it—scars that marked her on the inside and out.

She cleared her throat and called, "Come in!"

The door swung open. Aaron "Deuce" Porter stood on the other side of the threshold. His green gaze swept between them. "Didn't mean to interrupt anything." His voice was low.

"You're not," Rachel said flatly.

Deuce's lips twisted a bit. Deuce had been with the EOD for years—long before Rachel had come aboard. She'd worked several missions with him and learned quickly why the brown-haired agent had earned the moniker of Deuce.

The man could blend like no other. Undercover missions were his specialty. He often joked that he hadn't been born with just one face—but two.

Deuce. He could be two people in an instant, and had been, on missions in Rio, South Africa and the Middle East. He could drop an accent, change his walk, even change all of his mannerisms in an instant.

Two men—in one lethal body.

"Mercer briefed me on the case," he said as he came inside. He closed the door behind him. "I'm supposed to provide backup for your team." His smile faded. "Seems a reporter is getting a little too close on this one."

"Yes..." Dylan sighed out his answer. "But Cooper is working on her."

Now Deuce did laugh. "Well, Cooper has always had a way with the ladies."

Rachel's eyes narrowed.

"Love 'em and leave 'em," Deuce said. "If anyone can get the reporter under control, I'm sure it will be him."

Rachel's hands clenched into fists. "I think you're underestimating this woman. A little seduction isn't going to put her off track."

"Well, if that doesn't work—" Deuce's shoulders straightened "—option number two is a whole lot less pleasant for her. According to Mercer, the woman isn't to interfere in EOD business. Stopping her is a priority, even if we have to use containment."

Containment? On a civilian?

Mercer must really be worried. They hadn't crossed that line, not since—

Rachel cut off the thought. She didn't want to go into the darkness of her past. Not then.

But Dylan was staring straight at her, and she knew that she'd given herself away.

Sometimes she worried that Dylan was coming to know her too well.

And that scared her to death.

"SOMEONE'S BEEN WATCHING YOU?" Cooper repeated carefully. He made sure his expression reflected surprise. "Are you sure about that?"

"Yes, I am," she told him. "You think I don't know when I'm being tailed? I could feel someone following me for the past day, shadowing me. But every time I turned around..." Her breath blew out. "No one was there."

He made himself say, "Maybe because no one *was* there."

She shot to her feet. "Look, I'm trying to hire you, okay? You don't have to believe me in order to take the case."

"I thought you wanted us to be partners—"

Her dark eyes flashed at him. "I'm going to *pay* my partner for protection."

She was really afraid. He rose to his feet, slowly uncurling his body until he towered over her. "Are you sure nothing else has happened?"

Her lips pressed together then she said, "I think he was in my apartment."

Hell.

"My computer... At first I thought it was just some kind of glitch, but I had a tech I know take a look at it. He said my files were deliberately corrupted."

"Maybe you got a virus—"

"I've got top-of-the-line virus protection software. Whatever was done to my system, it was done by a professional."

Sydney definitely counted as a professional.

"All of the data that I'd had on that computer, all of the files on Archer and Lockwood—they were destroyed." She lifted her chin and her gaze glinted. "It's a good thing I had backups, because if I hadn't, I'd be in serious trouble with my boss."

His fingers locked around her shoulders. "You have backup files?"

For a second, she almost looked insulted. No, she *did* look insulted. "I'm not an amateur. This is what I do. I work these cases. I help *solve* the crimes that cops have to let go cold."

Why?

"Someone was in my place," she said again, dogged. "I know he was there."

"*How?* Did your alarm go off—"

"No, but my computer…it was moved. Just a few inches, but I could tell."

It figured she'd be that observant.

Gabrielle pulled away from him. "Look, if you won't help me, fine. I'll find someone else who will." Then she marched toward the door.

He stared up at the ceiling. This was so tangled. This was so—

The door opened.

In a flash, he rushed across the room and slammed the door shut. "I'll be your guard."

"Partner."

He turned her in his arms. "If that's the way you want to play it."

Gabrielle nodded. His body was flush against hers. Those kissable lips of hers were just inches away.

Focus.

The problem was that he *was* focusing, way too much on her.

"What will I owe you?"

His back teeth clenched. "My standard rate is five hundred a day." He totally pulled that number right out of the air.

Her eyes widened.

Too high.

"But I'll work out a deal with you," he rushed to say, because maybe this could work. If he stayed close to her—and he was planning to stay as close as he could possibly get—then he wouldn't have to worry about sneaking into her place again and destroying any more files. He'd be able to retrieve every bit of intel at the same time she did.

Even better, he'd be able to control the intel that she received.

"Deal?" Gabrielle whispered and she licked her lips.

His whole body stiffened. "Yeah, maybe I'll get my name mentioned in the byline of your story." Right. That would be the *last* thing he wanted.

He put his hands on either side of her head, flattening his palms against the door. He wanted her mouth beneath his. That one kiss hadn't been nearly enough to satisfy him.

It had just made him hungry for more.

"Of course, there is one other thing you can give me," Cooper said, aware that his voice had roughened even more than normal.

Her breath rushed out. Her hands rose to his chest even as bright flags of color stained her cheeks. "I am not—" she began angrily.

"Pie," he cut in. "I do believe there was a promise of cherry pie on the table." And if her cherry pie was half as good as her chocolate chip cookies had been, then he'd sure be one very lucky man.

She stopped pushing him. Her hands rested over his chest and seemed to burn right through the fabric of his T-shirt. "Oh. Right. Of course."

He smiled at her. She was so cute.

But dangerous.

Kiss her.

Instead, he dropped his hands and stepped away from her. "When does this partnership start?"

She glanced over his shoulder at the clock on the wall. "I'm really glad you agreed to my deal." Her head tilted. "Just how good are you at blending into the shadows?"

His lips twitched. "I get by." If she only knew.

"Good," Gabrielle said decisively, "because

I've got a lead for us to follow and our partnership starts right now."

HIS OLD FRIEND let him right inside the apartment. But then, he'd expected an easy entrance.

He'd also expected to see the haggard lines of grief on Van McAdams's face.

"Did you hear?" Van asked as he turned away. The guy left the door wide-open.

Van had better training than that. Much, much better.

"I saw the story on the news." His gloved fingers closed over the doorknob, and he pulled the door shut. He turned the lock quickly. There could be no time for any disturbances.

Van's shoulders were slumped as he headed toward the den. "What am I supposed to do now? Without Melanie, I don't have *anything*."

He pulled out his weapon. Slipped silently right up behind the man who mistakenly thought they were friends. "I guess you can join her. You can die."

Before Van could even turn to face him, it was too late. He'd attacked.

Van's body hit the floor seconds later.

The killer smiled. So easy. So incredibly—

Voices rose in the hallway. And one of those voices was familiar.

Cooper Marshall.

He stared down at the bloody knife in his hand and considered his options.

Chapter Four

"You're not coming in with me," Gabrielle said as she glanced over her shoulder. She kept her voice firm, authoritative. In this partnership, she was the one doing the paying, so it seemed fair that she got to be the one giving orders. Right? "You're to stay out here." She gestured toward him, then toward the small hallway. "Lurk. Make sure that no one else comes up here and tries to get in this apartment."

Because she was following a red-hot lead—one that she wasn't about to lose.

Kylie Archer had been murdered, and her boyfriend had also been killed in the same manner.

Now that Melanie Farrell was dead, would her boyfriend also follow suit? If the killer acted on the same time line, he could wait months to kill Melanie's lover.

That means I have time to talk to him, to warn him.

To save him?

Cooper didn't follow her lurk order. He stepped closer to her. "You need to tell me why we're here."

"I *did.*" On the motorcycle ride over, she'd yelled to him—*twice*—that she was following up on a lead. Her hand lifted and rapped against the apartment's door. She'd called and said she was coming by. The guy had been home an hour ago.

"A boyfriend," he said.

Still not lurking.

"I talked to Melanie's friend at work. Melanie's family didn't know about the guy, but if you're in deep with someone, the best friend *always* knows." It was a woman's rule. "Melanie called once and had Trish pick her up from this place. I did a little dot connecting, and I found the single guy in the apartment building who fit his description." A guy who was still not answering the door. "And voilà, I got him!"

"You got him," Cooper repeated, voice roughening.

She nodded but froze when she heard the distinct sound of glass shattering. That sound had come from *inside* the apartment.

Her fingers curled around the doorknob and she jerked, hard. "Mr. McAdams!"

Cooper stiffened.

"Van McAdams!" Gabrielle yelled. "It's Gabrielle Harper. We spoke earlier! Please, open up."

Cooper grabbed her shoulders and pushed her away from the door. In the next instant, he had a gun in his hands.

He'd just yanked that thing right out of his ankle holster, and he had it aimed at the door.

"What are you doing?" Gabrielle whispered, horrified. Her gaze flew down the hallway. "You can't just pull out a gun!"

"Two dead bodies, that's what I've found since I've been hanging out with you. I'm not in the mood for body number three." He squared his shoulders and called out, "Van, open the damn door, or I will bust my way inside."

The door didn't open.

Gabrielle started counting in her head. *One, two, thr—*

Cooper kicked the door open and rushed inside. He'd only taken about five steps when he froze—then dropped to the floor.

Because there was a man on the floor, a man sprawled in a pool of blood.

"Call an ambulance!" Cooper barked. He grabbed for the man, rolled him over.

Gabrielle flinched when she saw the man's neck. Fumbling, she yanked out her phone and managed to dial 911.

"Don't do this," Cooper growled. *"Don't."* Blood poured through his fingers as he tried to staunch the wound on the man's neck.

The man—Van McAdams?—his eyelids twitched.

He's still alive.

"What is the nature of your emergency?" the cool voice on the other end of the line asked Gabrielle.

"A man's been attacked! He's dying, please, get help here, now!" She threw out the address even as she tried to get closer to Cooper. His head had bent. His ear was right above the wounded man's mouth.

Surely McAdams couldn't talk with that kind of wound.

"We have an ambulance en route, ma'am," the operator told her.

"Get more than an ambulance!" She fired back. "Call Detective Lane Carmichael! He needs to get here, too."

"Gabrielle!" Cooper snapped out her name.

She blinked.

"I need you to put pressure on the wound." A muscle jerked in his jaw. "I have to search the apartment. The SOB who did this…he could still be here."

The breaking glass… Her gaze flew to the floor. There was no glass around McAdams. Someone else had made that sound.

"Gabrielle!" he snapped again.

She jumped to his side.

He positioned her hands. "Keep the pressure on him. Van, you look at her, okay? You stay with her."

Van wasn't looking at her. He wasn't looking at anyone.

Cooper surged to his feet. He had his gun with him as he ran down the hallway.

"It's okay," Gabrielle lied to the man who didn't even seem to be breathing. "Help's coming. You're going to make it. Just keep fighting. Stay with me."

Blood. So much blood.

It reminded her of another night.

No, don't go there. All of the scenes had reminded her—too much—of her past.

But…this scene… Her eyes were on the blood. Her breath froze in her lungs. Had Van…written something in the blood? It looked as if he had. An *E*. An *O*.

She squinted as she tried to make out the last letter. *D?*

What in the world was an EOD?

"Van, please, stay with me," she whispered to him as her hands pressed against his wound.

She leaned toward him, and felt something press into her knee. Her gaze darted from Van's pale face to the pool of blood.

Metal was there. Glinting. Rectangular in shape.

A dog tag?

A military dog tag. Its chain was broken.

When the killer cut his neck, he cut Van's dog tag right off him.

"Stay with me," she said again, but this time, she was begging because this man—he was the key. He could tell her the identity of the killer. He could solve all the crimes.

If he just lived.

THE BEDROOM WINDOW had been smashed. The shattered glass had fallen—a bit inside the room, but most had flown outside.

Cooper tried to lift the window.

Stuck.

So the killer had just improvised. When he heard Gabrielle at the door, he'd busted his way to freedom.

Cooper shoved his head outside and glanced below. There was no sign of the killer. He'd gotten away.

Again.

Van McAdams. They'd worked a case together over in Paris. Van was a good guy, quick to smile, slow to anger. Always cool under fire.

And now he's dying.

"Cooper!" Gabrielle yelled.

He knew what that yell meant. Cooper raced down the hallway as fast as he could, but he was too late. He'd been too late from the beginning.

By the time that the glass shattered, the killer had done his work.

Gabrielle looked up at him, tears glinting in her beautiful eyes. She was crying for a man she'd never met before that night.

His guts were tearing open because he *knew* Van. They'd laughed together, talked about their lives, women.

Van had been hoping to…

Marry. He'd had a girl that he'd been seeing for years.

Cooper put his hands on Van. He worked frantically to try and bring the guy back.

My girl...she hated all the traveling that I did, the secrecy. But things are going to change. I'm gettin' out of the EOD. I'm going to have a life. With her. Van's Mississippi drawl had rolled through the words and so had his determination to have his happiness.

But he hadn't gotten his life and that happily-ever-after dream.

"She was his girlfriend, wasn't she?" Cooper asked, his voice flat. He hadn't been able to find a link between Melanie Farrell and the EOD, because there wasn't a link. Not anymore.

Van had left the organization for her. So no one at the EOD had known about her.

His gaze fell on the message that had been written in blood. Every muscle in his body stiffened.

No, someone at the EOD knew. Someone damn well knew.

His boot slid out, smearing the blood and hiding the final message that Van had left behind.

Footsteps thundered outside of the apartment.

Help had finally arrived.

Too late.

"YOU DON'T LOOK like a killer."

Gabrielle's head whipped up at Detective Lane Carmichael's low voice. She was at the police station, in the *interrogation* room of all places.

She'd been the one to call Lane, but when he'd swung in with his cavalry, she'd found herself in police custody.

"You *know* I'm not a killer, Lane."

His lips compressed. "Maybe I don't know nearly as much about you as I thought, and I certainly don't know anything about the new guy you've got with you."

Lane had separated her from Cooper as soon as they arrived at the station. "Where is he?" Gabrielle demanded instead of responding to Lane's jibe.

Lane pulled up a chair and stared back at her. "Van McAdams is in the morgue, but you knew that, right? He was dead when you called for help."

Bile rose in her throat. "He wasn't dead then.

He was trying to talk." An impossible task, considering what had been done to him.

"Giving you a last-minute message, was he?" Lane asked.

She thought of the letters that she'd seen in the blood. Her eyes squeezed closed. "Look, I know you saw what he wrote. Despite this crazy act right now, you're a decent cop." Actually, a good cop. Maybe he was jealous. She didn't really know what his deal was. But there'd been a definite edge in his voice when he referred to the "new guy." "You're a—"

He grabbed her arm. "What are you talking about? What did McAdams write?"

Her eyes flew open. "I-in the blood. He tried to write a message. If you didn't see it, if one of the techs didn't, your guys are just getting sloppy."

He glared at her. "There was no message in the blood."

"Yes," she said, voice adamant, "there was." There had been no missing it.

"Then tell me...what did it say?"

Gabrielle licked her too dry lips. "There were three letters. I think...I think it was an *E*, an *O* and a *D*."

His brows shot up. "What is that supposed to mean?"

She didn't know, but Gabrielle intended to find out. "They could be the killer's initials or perhaps even the first three letters in his name." *Maybe you need to do your job and figure it out.*

But he just shook his head grimly. "You report the stories, Gabrielle. You aren't supposed to get in the middle of them. I told you this before. What you're doing is too dangerous."

Yes, he had told her that before: same song and dance, different day. The fact that he kept trying to control what she did…no, the fact that he kept trying to change her and make her into someone else—a girl who played things safely—*that* had been why their short-lived relationship had crashed and burned.

Lane exhaled slowly. "If you aren't careful, you could find yourself caught in the sights of a killer."

Then he shoved away from the table, stalked to the door, and he left her there.

Just…left her.

But the image of Van McAdams stayed with her, tightening her stomach and seeming to squeeze her heart. *I'm so sorry. I wish that I'd arrived sooner.*

Because seeing him like that, actually still alive—it was just like the night she'd found her father.

He'd been alive, too, when she first burst into her home. He'd been hurt so badly. She'd wanted to save him.

She'd only been able to watch him die.

A tear slid down her cheek as her shoulders hunched.

THE INTERROGATION WAS a joke. Like *this* was supposed to intimidate him? Being shut in a twelve-by-nine-foot room with a cup of water and air blowing on him, all nice and cool and comfortable?

This was like a vacation for him.

The door opened. The detective stalked inside. Lane Carmichael.

Carmichael's face was tight and angry, his eyes snapping. Ah, bad cop at his finest.

If Cooper hadn't been mourning McAdams, he could have appreciated the detective's performance. As it was, he felt annoyed. And he was ready to leave.

I need to meet up with my team.

"What was in the blood?" Detective Carmichael fired at him.

Cooper shook his head.

"Gabrielle said the victim wrote a final message in his own blood." Carmichael slapped his hands on the table and leaned toward Cooper. "What was the message?"

"I didn't see a message." He had a job to do. He'd sworn to protect the EOD. *I'm sorry, Gabrielle.*

"So Gabrielle is imagining things?" Carmichael asked. "Is that what you're saying?"

"I'm saying I didn't see anything." He'd hoped that she hadn't seen those letters. But maybe she hadn't been able to make them out clearly, and even if she had, Gabrielle wouldn't understand the message that McAdams had left behind.

"I don't trust you," Carmichael growled out the words. Red stained his cheeks. "I've been looking into your background, and you know what—"

The door flew open behind the detective. It banged against the wall with a thud. "Orders just came down," a sharp voice barked. "Marshall is free to go."

Carmichael's mouth dropped open in shock. Then he whirled and sputtered, "But, Captain, I was just—"

"Orders came down," the captain said, her voice brooking no argument. "He's free to go."

Cooper pushed back his chair. The captain glanced over his way, and her gray eyes narrowed. "You must know plenty of secrets about this city, Mr. Marshall," she murmured, "seeing as how the DA personally called me and said that you needed to be released."

Because his boss had no doubt made a fast call to the DA. Cooper inclined his head toward the captain. "When I leave, I'll be taking Ms. Harper with me."

But Carmichael was already shaking his head. "I've got more questions for Gabrielle."

"Then you can ask them tomorrow," Cooper responded, his own voice roughening. He could remember the glimmer of tears in Gabrielle's eyes. She'd been hurting and—*she needs me.* "She's been through hell, and I'm taking her home." He wasn't looking for permission from the cops. He was telling them what would happen.

If they wanted to discover just how much pull he had in D.C., then they'd try to stop him from taking Gabrielle out of that station.

After a brief hesitation, the captain inclined her head. The lights glinted off the dark red color. "Of course, Ms. Harper is free to go. Detective Carmichael will follow up with her tomorrow."

The detective's eyes were angry slits.

"Thank you," Cooper said as he marched through the open doorway. Then he turned to the left. He'd seen the other interrogation room when he'd been so…firmly…escorted into the station.

He shoved open that door.

Gabrielle was wiping at her cheeks. *Wiping away tears.* His chest ached. "It's time to go."

She glanced up at him.

When she cried, her face should have gone all splotchy. She shouldn't have looked even more beautiful with her gleaming eyes and trembling lips.

But she did.

He opened his hand to her.

Gabrielle pushed back her chair and nearly ran to him. "I didn't want him to die! I didn't—"

"It's okay," he said, trying to soothe her.

The soothing didn't work. Gabrielle shook her head. "I told McAdams that he could be in danger. I warned him that the killer could be targeting him next." Her gaze searched his. "Why didn't he listen?"

Because he trusted the wrong person.

That was what the man's final message had been about. He'd opened the door to another EOD agent. Someone he'd thought he could safely admit to his apartment as a colleague or a friend.

But when McAdams had turned his back, that friend had attacked him.

Cooper wrapped his arm around Gabrielle and turned for the door.

He wasn't particularly surprised to see Carmichael blocking the exit. As usual, the detective was glaring.

"Gabrielle told me that you both heard the sound of glass shattering…" Carmichael began.

Cooper nodded. He could confirm that part.

"You kicked in the door," Carmichael continued, pointing at Cooper, "and when you searched the place, you realized that the perp had broken the window and escaped?"

"Yes," Cooper snapped.

"Tell me how the hell he did that," Carmichael demanded. "He was four floors up. There was no fire escape. Am I supposed to believe the guy flew out of there?"

Cooper's hold tightened on Gabrielle. "The bricks were rough on that side of the building. Just as they were thrusting out a little too much at Lockwood's place. For a man with the right skills, getting out would almost be too easy. Scaling down would be just like rock climbing."

The detective stepped aside.

"Let's go," Cooper said into Gabrielle's ear. She was too pale.

They'd taken two steps past the detective when Carmichael mused, "The right skills… Tell me, Marshall, do you happen to possess those skills?"

Yes. "I'm not your killer, and you know it. Gabrielle's my alibi—"

"And you're hers, yes, I *know* that. But I wasn't asking if you killed the man. I was asking if you *could* have gotten out of that apartment the same way that the killer did."

Gabrielle had stopped walking. She stared up at Cooper, waiting.

There was no point in lying. "Yes, I could have. I would have been down that wall and away from the scene in less than a minute. *Just like the perp was.*"

Then, before the cop could ask him any other questions, Cooper took Gabrielle toward the front of the station.

His motorcycle wasn't around—one of his teammates would take care of it for him—so he directed Gabrielle into the first cab that he saw.

They raced away from the station.

He glanced back and wasn't surprised to see a dark SUV slip behind the cab. He knew that his boss had been the one pulling the strings to get him out of the station, and Mercer would want an accounting of the night's activities right away.

But Mercer would have to wait.

Because there was someone else who needed him first.

His arms tightened around Gabrielle.

SO MUCH BLOOD.

Before she'd been escorted to the interrogation room at the station, she'd washed and washed her hands, but Gabrielle swore that she could still feel the blood on her skin.

She'd watched Van McAdams die, and she hadn't been able to do *anything* to help him.

Just like before.

"It's not your fault."

They were in front of the brownstone. The cab's wheels rolled away, leaving them alone out there. The night was hot, stifling, and Gabrielle thought she could still smell the overwhelming scent of blood.

He opened the door and led her inside.

When he paused, she didn't stop. Gabrielle headed straight for the stairs.

But Cooper caught her hand, stilling her on the second step. "You think I don't know what you're doing?"

Right then, she was trying to run. "Can't be in fighting form all the time," she murmured. "Sometimes…sometimes we all need to crash." That was exactly what she wanted to do. She wanted to get inside her apartment where she could fall apart and no one would see her break.

He put his foot on the bottom stair. "Whatever you need, I can give you."

She shook her head.

Cooper turned her back to face him. His hand lifted, and his fingers curled around her chin as he stared into her eyes. "I can keep you safe. You can crash, you can fall, and I'll be there to pick you right back up."

Her lips trembled. She caught her lower lip between her teeth because she didn't want him seeing that weakness.

Just hold it together a little longer.

But McAdams—those last, terrible moments—had stirred up memories of her own past that she just couldn't shut out any longer.

There was a reason she took the cold cases. A reason she tried so hard to find justice for the ones who had been forgotten.

"Fall into me," he told her again. "I'm here."

When had anyone else ever said something like that to her? She'd stood on her own for so long, Gabrielle couldn't remember what it was like to have someone else there when the storm hit.

She found herself nodding. "Come…upstairs with me?" So she wouldn't be alone when the crash hit.

Then Gabrielle turned. She headed slowly up that staircase, and Cooper was right behind her. She could feel the reassuring heat and strength of his body following hers.

She opened the door to her apartment, flipped on the lights, reached for the alarm—

And realized that her place had been trashed.

Couch cushions were cut. Furniture overturned. Her files were scattered across the floor.

"Get back!" Cooper's low snarl. He didn't wait for her to comply. He grabbed her shoulders and pushed her back behind him.

He had his gun in his hand again. She didn't even remember him getting that weapon back from the cops at the precinct. While he pushed her back, Cooper stepped inside her place.

No. She grabbed his arm. “He could still be here.” Wasn’t that what they’d feared at McAdams’s place? That the killer was there?

“I hope he is,” Cooper whispered back.

Then he advanced.

Fear twisted within her, but she wasn’t about to stay in that hallway by herself. Maybe *that* was the killer’s plan. Divide and conquer. So when Cooper stalked forward, she leapt right after him.

Her hands fisted around her keys—and the mace attached to that keychain. Having her own weapon made her feel a little bit better.

Until they got to her bedroom.

And she saw the clothing that had been slashed. The other room…it had almost looked as if someone was searching for something in her den. But this—this was just destruction.

Her pillows had been slit open. Feathers covered the floor. Her sheets were cut, her mattresses sliced.

Her dresser mirror was smashed.

All of her drawers had been yanked out and tossed. Her breath heaved in at the sight.

Rage. She could feel it in the room.

Cooper’s body stiffened, but he didn’t speak. He kept searching her home—checking the closets, the bathroom.

No one was there.

The intruder was long gone.

Gabrielle found herself standing in the living room, gazing around with dazed eyes. *Everything* that she'd valued was gone.

Cooper was on his phone. Probably calling the police for her. *Again.*

She rubbed chilled arms. The cold wasn't just on the surface, though, it went bone deep.

Cooper shoved his phone back into his pocket. He'd already holstered his weapon.

You can fall into me. She wanted to fall right then, but Gabrielle was afraid that if she did, she'd never be able to get up again.

"I told you," she said and was surprised by how eerily calm her voice sounded. "Someone was watching me."

"You were right." His eyes blazed with a barely banked fury. She should be feeling a similar fury, but she wasn't. That coldness seemed to be cloaking all of her emotions.

"I called in a favor," he told her. She couldn't look away from his eyes. She didn't want to look anywhere else. *Everything is gone.* "I've got a team coming over here. If the SOB left any prints, any evidence, we'll find him."

That seemed…odd to her. "You didn't call Carmichael?"

"He'll be informed." His fingers curled around

her arms. "Right now, I want you to come downstairs with me. You're going to be staying at my place tonight."

His place. Her eyes widened. "What if—what if he did this to your apartment, too?"

"I don't think—"

She pushed past him and ran down the stairs. Cooper was working with her now. What if the intruder had realized that? What if he'd destroyed Cooper's place, too?

Breath heaving, she staggered to a stop at Cooper's door. He was beside her. Always, moving so fast. He unlocked his door. Hit the lights.

Untouched.

The intruder had just gone after her. He'd just destroyed *her* home.

"I'm glad," she whispered as her shoulders slumped. "I didn't want him hurting you...because I pulled you into this mess."

He swore and tugged her closer to him.

"I know it's related, it has to be," she said. She wasn't going to ignore the facts, even though they terrified her. "It's him. The killer. He knows I was at McAdams's place. He could have been there, watching us from the outside when the police arrived." A crowd of people had gathered on the street.

He could have been right there.

Her heart pounded in a double-time rhythm.

"He knows who I am, where I live. And getting hauled into the station by Carmichael tonight…" She swallowed. "That just might have saved my life."

Because maybe the perp's knife wouldn't have just been used on her furniture and clothes.

He could have used it on me.

Chapter Five

Cooper shut his apartment door. Gabrielle was inside, showering, and he had a few minutes to spare.

Rachel and Dylan Foxx were already waiting outside for him—along with a sweeper crew. He jerked his head, and the crew hurried upstairs. If the killer had left evidence behind, they'd find it.

"The local cops?" he asked. Because Carmichael would find out about tonight's events, sooner or later.

The EOD wanted that discovery to be *later*.

"Our team won't leave evidence behind. The detective will be called in once we're finished," Rachel said smoothly.

Because before the local authorities took over, they had to make sure nothing had been left to implicate the EOD.

His hands clenched into fists as his gaze met Dylan's stare. "He's targeting her."

"That doesn't fit." It was Rachel who replied. "He's going after EOD agents—"

"Their girlfriends," Cooper said flatly. "He kills the girlfriends, the lovers, first. Then he goes after the agents." It was the rogue's pattern. "He knows these men, knows them better than we do." *Because he was hiding behind the mask of a friend.* "And maybe he thinks that Gabrielle saw something, that she knows *something* about him, because that SOB destroyed her home."

He wouldn't even allow himself to think about what might have happened if Gabrielle had *been* home when the rogue attacked.

"Are you sure," Dylan asked, voice quiet and gaze steady, "that she doesn't know more? She was the one who found out about Van, right? Long before anyone in-house knew he was connected to Melanie Farrell."

"Someone in-house knew." He hadn't been given a chance to reveal this yet. "The last thing Van did was leave a message for me, in his own blood. *EOD.* That's what he wrote." McAdams had just been confirming what they already knew—

The killer terrorizing D.C. was one of their own.

"Did the cops see that message?" Dylan demanded as his face tensed.

"No, I took care of it." And that didn't sit well

with him. He'd destroyed evidence. "But Gabrielle saw it."

Rachel and Dylan shared a long look.

"What?" Cooper snapped.

"She's a reporter," Rachel reminded him with a raised brow.

"I *know* what she is."

"She's not going to forget what she saw. That woman will dig and dig until she figures out what the EOD truly is."

Not possible.

"You have to stop her." Dylan's firm order. Dylan was the team leader on this case. The former SEAL had been working with the EOD much longer than Cooper had. "Throw her off the scent, give her another lead, but stop her from focusing on the EOD."

Easier said than done. "Right now, my goal is to keep her safe." Even as he said the words, he realized they were true. It wasn't about finding out what Gabrielle knew any longer. Not about getting close to any intel that she might possess.

He wanted to make sure that she didn't get hurt. That the rogue didn't come within ten feet of her again.

And I want to make sure that if she ever does fall, I'm right there to catch her.

The thought rushed through him.

Changed him.

Then he heard the rustle of footsteps behind him. "She's coming," he whispered. Gabrielle would be looking for him, and she'd want to know what was happening upstairs.

The door opened behind him bare seconds later. He glanced over his shoulder.

Her long hair was wet. Slicked back, it accentuated her high cheekbones and her wide, dark eyes.

She'd put on one of his old T-shirts. It seemed to swallow her delicate shoulders, and she'd worked some kind of magic to get a very faded pair of his running shorts to fit her.

Her bare toes—adorned with bright red polish—curled against the hard wood floor. "I hope you don't mind," Gabrielle said softly, "but I didn't have anything else to wear."

Because the rogue had destroyed everything she had.

Bastard.

"I don't mind at all." The words came out too gruff. Too rough. He cleared his throat and tried again, saying, "I can go out and get some more clothes for you, if you tell me your size."

Actually, he already knew her size. It was in the nice, tidy dossier that the EOD had given him.

"Why don't you let me make a run?" Rachel interrupted.

Gabrielle's gaze slid to her.

"Most of the stores will be opening in a few

hours," Rachel added. "I can get the clothes for you, no problem."

Gabrielle hesitated. Then she cocked her head as her gaze slid between Rachel and Dylan, and the top of the stairs. "I'm sorry...what are you all doing here? I thought the cops were coming to investigate."

"My name's Dylan Foxx, and I am the cops, sort of," Dylan said as he offered his hand to her.

Gabrielle took his hand. "Sort of?"

"I work for the government," Dylan explained. Cooper was surprised by that truth. But then Dylan continued, twisting fact and fiction as he explained, "I have a crew that specializes in crime scene investigation for Uncle Sam. They're upstairs now, and as soon as they're done, I'll be turning the results over to—" he glanced at Cooper as if for confirmation "—a Detective Carmichael?"

Cooper realized that Dylan was still holding Gabrielle's hand. What was up with that? He maneuvered her away from Dylan. Dylan had a tendency to be a little too slick with the ladies.

"Do you work for the government, too?" Gabrielle asked Rachel.

Rachel nodded. "I'm Dylan's associate."

Gabrielle fiddled with the bottom of Cooper's shirt. "By any chance, have either of you ever heard of the EOD?"

Cooper's heart slammed into his chest.

Rachel frowned. "The what?"

At the same moment, Dylan shook his head. "No, can't say that I have. Why? What is it?"

Gabrielle turned toward Cooper. "It was written in the blood at the crime scene. You saw it, didn't you?"

He *hated* to do it, but Cooper shook his head. "No, sweetheart, I didn't."

She blinked. "But…it was there. Carmichael said he didn't see it, but you had to—"

"I didn't," he made himself say again.

Her gaze fell. "I saw it," she said softly, determinedly. "*EOD.* Clear as day. That was McAdams's last message, and I'm going to figure out what it means."

No, you can't find out.

Her gaze touched his once more. "I'm going to call my editor at the *Inquisitor.* I want to publish an account of everything that happened. Somewhere out there, someone knows either who or what the EOD is."

That couldn't happen. There was no way that he could let her publish what she'd seen.

Dylan's gaze met Cooper's. He easily read the order in the other man's eyes.

Cooper inclined his head.

"When your team finishes," Cooper said, "give us a report."

"Of course," Dylan agreed. His attention shifted to Gabrielle. "I'm sorry we had to meet under these circumstances."

"So am I." Her lips twisted into a weak smile. "But if you and your team can help me to find the man who broke into my place, I'd sure appreciate it."

"We'll do everything we can," Dylan told her. He backed away.

Rachel lingered. There were shadows in her eyes as she studied Gabrielle. "It doesn't seem safe," Rachel suddenly blurted.

Dylan frowned at her.

"The story that you're following…all of the people that are winding up dead." Rachel exhaled on a shaky breath. "Do you have family who live outside of D.C.? Friends? Maybe you should leave until the police catch this guy."

"His first victim was killed four months ago," Gabrielle said. "Four months. The police haven't caught him yet, and I'm not the type to run and hide and just *hope* that things change."

"Even if staying puts you in harm's way?" Rachel pressed.

Gabrielle's shoulder brushed against Cooper. "I've got my own bodyguard. I trust him to keep me safe."

Don't put so much trust in me.

The mission had started so easily.

But right then, he hated the lies that he'd told to Gabrielle.

Rachel got the sizes for Gabrielle's clothes and she promised to be back first thing in the morning with the items. When she started to leave, Gabrielle reached out and gave the other woman a quick hug.

Surprise rippled across Rachel's face.

"Thank you," Gabrielle told her as she eased back. "After what happened, just knowing that clothes are coming—" This time, her smile was full and real. "It may sound crazy, but it means a lot to me. Actually, it means everything. This guy isn't going to stop me. He won't intimidate me. I'm going to get justice for his victims."

Because that was what Gabrielle did, Cooper realized. She didn't go after the criminals because she wanted attention or glory. She did it for the victims.

So they wouldn't be forgotten.

Gabrielle slipped back into the apartment.

He turned to follow her, but stopped when he saw Rachel glaring at him.

That glare would have melted a lesser man.

He leaned toward Rachel, acting as if he were giving her a hug. "What is it?" Cooper whispered.

Her body was stiff and tense against his. "She deserves better than this," Rachel hissed.

Better than you.

Yes, she did. Jaw locking, he followed Gabrielle inside his apartment, and he wondered just what he'd have to do in order to stop her from telling the world about the EOD.

BRUCE MERCER SAT in his office. His fingers tapped on his desk, a slow, steady rhythm as he listened to Dylan Foxx's update.

The agent was rambling, unusual for him. That rambling meant—

"You found nothing in the reporter's place," Bruce said.

Finally, Dylan stopped his ramble about fingerprint dusting and DNA analysis. Dylan gave a quick nod. "The fact that they didn't find anything is significant, sir."

No, it wasn't. "We already knew one of ours was behind the kills. It only stands to reason that if he didn't leave a trace at the other scenes then he'd be just as careful at Gabrielle Harper's place." The EOD agents were the deadliest and the most covert in the U.S.

Some in his unit were even called Shadow Agents—men and women who were so good at infiltrating enemy camps and carrying out their dangerous missions that they more closely resembled shadows than humans.

You didn't hear a shadow, didn't feel it. Didn't even realize it was there—until it was too late.

"Cooper stopped the cops from seeing that Van had written *EOD* as an identifier for his killer," Dylan said. "But he was too late to prevent Gabrielle from seeing the message. She told us that she was going to print that info in the *Inquisitor*."

"No, she isn't." Even if he had to shut that place down, he'd make sure her report never saw the light of day. He wasn't going to risk the lives of innocent agents. Not that it wouldn come to that point. He had faith in one man. "Cooper will stop her. He'll find a way to convince her that isn't the right tactic to use."

"You sound awful certain..."

"I am." Bruce's attention turned to the fat stack of manila folders in front of him. "I've called in a profiler." One that he'd handpicked from the FBI. He didn't usually let the Bureau nose around his cases, but this was a different situation.

Right then, the EOD could actually *use* someone from the outside. A fresh pair of eyes, an unbiased observer, was exactly what he needed.

He had high hopes for Noelle Evers.

She'd better not disappoint him.

"Do you know," Mercer asked the other man, curious, "how many agents we've had at the EOD in the past fifteen years?"

Dylan shook his head.

Of course, he didn't know. That intel was classified.

"When agents leave, we do our best to keep tabs on them, but the truth of the matter is this… they leave because they want to vanish. They want to start new lives and not be hunted by their enemies."

They tried to make their pasts disappear.

"But these men and women aren't like everyone else. They're the deadliest foes you could ever cross. I trained them. I brought them into this life." His fisted hand slammed down on the files. "So that means I'm the one responsible for this killer—a man who started on this dark path because he wanted to hurt *me*."

They'd first become aware of the rogue months back, when inside information on Mercer had been leaked to one of his oldest and most powerful enemies. Anton Devast had learned about Mercer's daughter. He'd tried to kill her in order to get revenge on Mercer.

A life for a life.

In the end, Devast had been the one to die.

With Devast's death, the rogue had spiraled even more out of control. The deaths had started then. More than just what the press knew about. More than just what the intrepid Gabrielle Harper had discovered.

With Van's death, they'd now lost four agents.

Four.

All within the past six months.

"Profilers are supposed to tell which men and women are killers," Dylan spoke slowly, bringing Mercer's attention back to him. "But here, that's what we all are."

Mercer shook his head. "No, Foxx, you've got that wrong. You're soldiers. You're heroes. The profiler is looking for a monster, someone pretending to be just like you." Someone adept at hiding his true self.

Mercer pushed back in his chair. His gaze cut to the right, to the window that overlooked D.C. "I never thought the biggest threat I'd face would come from within the organization that *I* made." With blood, sweat, tears. He'd sacrificed so much for the EOD. Even his family.

I'm sorry, Marguerite. His wife had been one of the first that he lost—the first, and the one that still made him feel like he was missing half of his heart.

How much longer? It wasn't the first time he'd wondered that question. How much longer could he truly sit at the helm of the EOD?

Maybe he was getting too old for this mess. Maybe he should be the one looking for a way out.

I need someone else to take over the reins.

Because the idea of escape could sure tempt any agent.

But Mercer couldn't allow his legacy to be destroyed. "We'll find him," he vowed. He wasn't going out—not yet.

Not like this.

When he left, it would be on his terms. It wouldn't be due to some twisted killer who'd decided to put EOD agents on his hit list.

The EOD had survived attacks before. Hell, agents had been targeted before. When you were the best out there, plenty of enemies would come gunning for you.

We stopped them before. We'll stop this SOB, too.

COOPER MARSHALL HAD taken in the reporter. He'd brought her into his apartment so that they could spend the night together.

How cozy.

The watcher stood outside of the brownstone. Dawn hadn't come yet, and the darkness concealed him as he stared at the building.

Last night, he'd also learned that Marshall had called in his team—Rachel Mancini and Dylan Foxx.

They were on his list, too. Another pair that would be destroyed.

But first he had to deal with the reporter. She'd

surprised him by getting too close, far closer than the EOD. He wouldn't underestimate her again.

He would use her.

A light was shining in Cooper's bedroom. He could see the shadows of two forms—Cooper and Gabrielle.

He smiled as he watched those shadows.

Oh, yes, Gabrielle would definitely be useful to him.

She would help him to destroy Cooper.

"YOU TAKE THE BED," Cooper said as he rolled back his shoulders and tried to keep his gaze off the long, golden expanse of Gabrielle's legs. "I'll bunk on the couch."

He turned away from her, away from those tempting legs.

"Sleep is going to be impossible, you know that, right?"

He glanced back over his shoulder at her. "You're exhausted. You've been up most of the night." *And been terrified the majority of that time.* "You need rest."

"And every time I even *think* about closing my eyes, guess what I see?" Those dark chocolate eyes were wide and on him. "It's not exactly an image that makes me want to hit the dream circuit."

Her fingers were trembling. Her body held too tightly, too stiffly.

He faced her once more. “The rush. You still have adrenaline spiking through you.”

Her hands fisted. “The shower didn’t exactly stop that. It didn’t do anything to calm me down.”

No. He took a step toward her. “I told you before, I can help with that.” Adrenaline still coursed through his own blood—adrenaline and fury. *The rogue had gone after her.*

Gabrielle shook her head. “I don’t want a drink. The whiskey didn’t work for me last time.”

Her lips were red and full, and that little quiver of her bottom lip made him want to kiss her, to feel that quiver beneath his own mouth. “Forget the drink,” he said, voice rumbling, “I’ve got something else in mind.”

Something that he’d needed, wanted…

He took another step toward her. She didn’t back away.

But her gaze did drop to his mouth.

“Cooper…”

He loved the way she said his name. Not with fear or hesitation but with need, a yearning to match his own.

His fingers slid under her chin. He tipped her head back. “Once wasn’t enough.” One kiss had done nothing but stir his appetite for her.

They were alone. Safe. Adrenaline could be turned into passion so easily.

His head lowered.

She rose onto her toes and her hands—now unclenched—pressed to his chest.

The first touch of his lips against hers was tentative. Easy. A hard task when the desire pumping through him was dark and demanding.

He wanted her on the bed. He wanted her naked. He wanted to hear her scream his name.

One step at a time.

Because before he got what he wanted, Cooper needed to seduce her.

Her mouth parted beneath his.

He took the kiss deeper. Swept his tongue past her lips and tasted her. Sweet. So sweet. She could easily become an addiction to him.

The kiss grew harder as the desire beat in his blood. His hand slipped from her chin and sank into the rich fullness of her hair.

The bed is so close.

He found himself backing her toward the bed. Still kissing her, only now the kiss was deep and hard and it still wasn't enough.

He wasn't sure he could get enough from her.

His mouth pulled from hers, and he began to kiss her neck. Her scent filled his nostrils. *Lilacs.* His aroused flesh pressed hard against the front of his jeans.

"I don't...do this..." Her voice was husky. Her nails bit through the fabric of his shirt. "I don't...I don't just jump into bed with men I don't know."

He stilled at that and looked at her. "You know me."

"I've lived upstairs from you for months." She licked her lips.

Need sharpened within him.

"But I don't *know* you. Who were you before you came here? You have secrets, Cooper. Sometimes, I can all but feel them between us."

He kissed her again, helpless to do anything else. He kissed her, took her mouth and wanted to take *her.*

The desire he felt for her was stronger than anything he'd experienced before. Cooper had enjoyed more than his share of lovers. He should be able to hold on to his control easily.

Instead, he could feel it shredding.

Because of her.

"There's nothing between us," he said, whispering the words against her mouth. "Right now, there's me and there's you, and nothing else matters."

Not the killer hunting them.

Not his secrets.

"Trust me," he told her. "I won't hurt you. You can count on me."

Her lashes lifted. Her eyes were so beautiful and deep. There were flecks of gold in the darkness of her eyes. As he looked into her eyes, he had the odd feeling that she was seeing into him. Seeing past the mask he wore for others and straight into his soul.

His chest ached.

She's not like the others.

Cooper kissed her once more, because he had to do it. Kissed her deep and savored her.

Then he stepped back. "When you do trust me enough, you let me know." The words were low, growling from him. "Because you will reach that point. You'll see that you can count on me, and I'll be here. When you're ready, I'll be here," he said again.

She stared back at him. Her lips were flushed, slightly swollen from his kiss. Her cheeks were stained red.

So. Beautiful.

He forced himself to offer her a smile. "And by here," he said quietly, "I mean the couch. Because I think you need some time." *Before you become mine.*

Once they crossed that line, there would be no going back.

She'd changed the rules for him. He didn't think Gabrielle realized just how intense things could become.

Before his control broke, Cooper headed for the door. His fingers curled around the knob.

"I've had one lover."

That stopped him.

"When I said that I didn't jump into bed, I meant it." Her words tumbled out. "I'm not looking to be a flavor of the week with you. I—"

"Sweetheart," he said this without glancing back at her. His control was barely hanging on. "You'd never be that." She was in a class all her own. "When we are together…" *Hell, yes, they would be.* "It's not going to be about anyone else. No one from your past, no one from mine. It's only going to be about us. About pleasure." He opened the door. "You'll trust me soon enough."

He left her, because if he stayed even a few moments more, they would be on the bed.

WHEN THE DOOR shut behind Cooper, Gabrielle's breath wheezed out.

Wow. She was…

Her eyes closed. She didn't think she was ready to handle Cooper Marshall.

She had the feeling that he was the kind of guy who just might be able to ruin her for all others.

When he'd been kissing her, when his big, strong hands had been on her, she'd wanted him to ruin her. She'd wanted him to do all kinds of things to her.

It hadn't been about the adrenaline. It had been about good, old-fashioned lust.

The only thing that had held her back? *Fear.*

She wasn't physically afraid of Cooper. Actually, she was sure he wouldn't hurt her like that at all.

Gabrielle was afraid of the way he made her feel. Out of control. Edgy. Wild.

Those feelings were dangerous.

Cooper Marshall was dangerous.

THE KILLER WATCHED as the light in Cooper's bedroom finally shut off. For a while there, those two shadows had gotten close.

Intimately close.

But then one form had left. Cooper.

Playing the gentleman. What a lie.

He was sure Cooper wouldn't keep up the act for long.

In his experience, Cooper wasn't exactly a man known for his patience. When Cooper saw something he wanted, he took it.

Just like I do.

He and Cooper had quite a great deal in common. That similarity was why they had worked well together in the field.

They'd battled side by side.

Cooper had even saved his life.

He should have let me die.

That had been Cooper's mistake. Now, death would come again. Only this time, Cooper would be the one to wind up in the pine box.

Chapter Six

"You can't do this," Cooper's voice rumbled as he leaned over Gabrielle's shoulder and glared at the computer screen. "If you publish this, it will be like waving a red flag right at the killer!"

Gabrielle glanced up and found him just inches away from her. Close enough to kiss.

No, no, do not go there.

She jerked her gaze away from his lips. "Other reporters have already scooped me on this case! I can't sit on the story any longer."

It was just past 9:00 a.m. She'd given up on the whole concept of sleep quickly enough, and when Rachel had appeared with fresh clothes—Gabrielle seriously owed that woman—she'd wasted no time in rushing down to the *Inquisitor*'s main office.

Her home computer might have been smashed, but she still had data on file at her workstation.

"No one else," he said slowly, seeming to force the words out as he glared at her, "is even mentioning anything about a message being written in blood. You can't—"

"I can," she cut him off. "I will."

His eyes narrowed to blue slits. "You're baiting the killer. You want him to come after you again, is that it?"

"I don't have a death wish." She hit Send on the file—it would be on her boss's computer instantly. With a story this big, she had to get Hugh's permission to publish. Hugh lived for breaking the big news. He'd probably give her the okay in five minutes flat.

"He was in your home."

Like she needed the reminder. "I want him stopped." She pushed to her feet.

He straightened and kept that hot, bright stare on her. "You think using yourself as bait is going to do that?"

"I'm not—"

"Harper!" Hugh's bellowing voice cut across the room. "My office. Now."

Wow. That hadn't even been two full minutes. The boss did like his stories. She brushed by Cooper, slid out of her cubicle, and hightailed it to Hugh's office. She heard Cooper following behind her, and she saw Penelope Finn's gaze cut appreciatively to him. Penelope was the lead entertainment reporter, and the woman was always, *always,* styled to perfection.

Penelope leapt to her feet as they passed her desk. She was wearing a body-hugging dress that matched her golden eyes, and she zeroed in on Cooper—literally blocking him with her body. "I don't think we've met," she said.

Gabrielle rolled her eyes. Typical Penelope. Gabrielle didn't slow down to rescue Cooper. He was a big boy; he could rescue himself. Besides, her boss stood in the doorway, glaring at her.

Hugh was wearing a stark white shirt that emphasized his coffee-cream skin. Hugh considered himself a master of style, and the guy had been known to charm his way into any and every closed-door meeting in D.C.

But, beneath the charm, a real bulldog lurked.

She loved that about him. After all, Hugh had been the one to teach her everything that she knew about reporting.

"No, we haven't met," Gabrielle heard Cooper say flatly to Penelope. "Sorry, but excuse me."

Then, before she could reach Hugh, Cooper's fingers closed around her shoulder.

Gabrielle glanced back.

"You can't go live with that story," he told her.

"No," Hugh said, voice still a bellow even though they were about five feet from him. "She can't."

The charm certainly wasn't in effect then.

Jaw dropping in surprise, Gabrielle whirled back toward her boss. "You're not serious."

"Dead serious." He jerked his thumb over his shoulder. "My office, Harper, now."

Definitely no charm.

She stumbled into his office.

Cooper tried to come with her.

Hugh stepped in his path. Cooper was at least a head taller and probably seventy-five pounds heavier than her boss, but Hugh still doggedly blocked his entrance as he studied the younger man.

"Who are you?" Hugh demanded. "And why are you in my newsroom?"

"I'm her partner," Cooper shot right back. "Where she goes, I go."

"Is that so?" Hugh let him in the office. His dark, assessing gaze raked over Cooper. "Protection, huh? A bodyguard?" He shut the door behind Cooper, sealing them all inside. "Good." He stomped toward his computer. "After what I just read, she can't be safe enough."

"Uh, *she* is right here!" Gabrielle barely managed to keep the words below a shout. "And what do you mean, Hugh? I can't publish the story? It's a *huge* story."

Hugh exhaled loudly. "When are you going to realize, there are more important things than stories? Your *life* is on the line here." He shook his dark head. "No, no, I'm not doing it. I'm not going to let you tell the killer you were minutes behind him last night—"

Gabrielle had to laugh at that. "He already knows. Why do you think he broke into my place?"

"Because you're the next target on his list?"

Hugh's words made her skin chill. "I'm not."

"You're smarter than that. You just don't want to admit it, because if you do, then you'll realize that you're neck deep in danger." He ran a hand over his chin. "We'll keep some of the article. The parts that *don't* yell 'Come and get me' to the killer."

Her article did not yell that.

"Get a confirmation from Carmichael that we're dealing with a serial, and we can lead with that. We'll give him a name, something flashy and scary like the City Stalker, and we'll—"

She could see red. Literally. "It's not about making this guy into a celebrity. It's about catching him!"

Hugh crossed his arms over his chest. "For me, it's about keeping my reporter safe. Change the story. Take out the part about the message that was written in blood—hell, the cops probably want that kept off the record anyway."

"But someone out there could know what the

message means!" This was insane. And this was not *Hugh Peters.* Not Hugh Print-It-All Peters.

"In its current form, this story will *not* be published at the *Inquisitor.*" His eyes, a shade darker than her own, pinned her. "This isn't your first rewrite, so just get back to your desk and take care of business."

She was missing something. "You've never backed down from a story before."

He swallowed. His gaze cut to a silent Cooper.

"Did someone…did someone contact you?" she asked. Crazy but…Hugh truly didn't back down from stories. "Hugh, do you know what the EOD actually is?"

"Bodyguard," Hugh muttered, "I'm going to insist that you step out of the room, right now."

"I'm not moving," Cooper said.

Her heart was about to burst out of her chest. *Hugh knows.* "Cooper, I want to talk to Hugh. It's just the two of us here. We'll be perfectly safe."

The faint lines near Cooper's eyes tightened.

"I'm the paying partner, remember?" she managed.

Uh-oh. *Wrong* thing to say. His eyes went glacial. "How could I forget?" He turned for the door. "I'll just go play watchdog from outside."

She hadn't meant to make him angry. She'd apologize, mend fences and do whatever. *After* she found out what Hugh was holding back from her.

The door clicked closed behind Cooper.

"Spill," she demanded.

Beads of sweat lined Hugh's forehead. "Are you sure your guard won't try to listen in?"

No, she wasn't sure of that at all. Actually, she expected him to at least attempt some good eavesdropping. Gabrielle would be rather disappointed in him if he didn't.

"What do you know? Tell me, Hugh. After what I've been through, I think I deserve to know."

He crooked his finger, motioning for her to come closer.

Frowning, she maneuvered toward him.

"You're in over your head," he whispered.

No way would Cooper be able to eavesdrop on that whisper.

"I've dealt with killers before." She tried to sound confident. Like fear wasn't a tight knot in her gut.

"If the killer is working with the EOD, then he's like no one you've ever faced before."

He knew.

"EOD…it's a business?" That hadn't been the initials for a person's name, but something else.

"No." He licked his lips. His gaze darted toward the shut door. "I've only heard whispers, because that's all anyone ever hears. No facts. No proof. Nothing that will ever make it into the press."

"Hugh." Impatience hardened his name. "You're talking in circles, and you're telling me nothing."

"The government."

Hugh had conspiracy theories—a lot of them. She sighed. So much for getting the truth—

"The EOD is a covert unit that works for Uncle Sam. Trained killers. Brutal, cold."

The killer who'd gone after Lockwood and the others had certainly been brutal. His prey hadn't even had time to fight back.

"I've never heard of the EOD." She'd been in Washington for seven years. She'd graduated college, then come to the big city.

"You wouldn't. They're so far off the radar, most civilians never know about them."

"But you heard whispers." An EOD agent. If the killer was as well trained as Hugh was saying, then scaling the side of the apartment should've been easy for him. Cooper had said that a man with the right skills would have no problem climbing down those bricks.

The right skills.

"A man came to me with a story once." Again, his gaze shifted to the door, and he kept his voice low. "He'd been kidnapped off some speck of an island in the Caribbean. He thought for sure his captors would kill him, but then rescue came."

"This story sounds like it had a happy ending—"

"All seven of his captors died. They were

taken out by *one* man. One. An EOD agent. The guy said the agent moved like a shadow, faster than anything he'd ever seen. Before his captors could fire their weapons, they were dead on the ground." He sucked in a deep breath. "That's what they are. Death."

"It sounds like the agent was saving him—"

"I did some poking around after that case. A message was delivered to me." His fingers shook. "One that convinced me I wanted to stay away from anything involving the EOD."

Hugh had been scared. No, he was *still* scared.

"I'm delivering the same message to you. You're one hell of a reporter. You're got more grit and determination than anyone else who's walked through the doors of the *Inquisitor*." His shoulders thrust back. "But I don't want to see you disappear, and the EOD can do that. They can make you vanish."

Her fingernails bit into her palms as her hands curled tightly. "The last thing Van McAdams did was leave that bloody message. You're telling me that the EOD had him killed? Killed his girlfriend? Killed Lockwood and Kylie Archer?"

"I'm saying that if *you* want to stay alive, then you need to forget about the EOD."

Like that was going to happen.

"I don't want you putting any more of a target on yourself. Your life isn't worth a headline."

Hugh was a good man. Sure, he blustered, he bulldozed, but he cared about the people who worked for him. He—

"If I have to, I'll bench you," he threatened. "I'll pull you off the crime beat and get you to help Penelope with the gala coming up at the White House."

"You wouldn't."

"To keep you alive, I would."

Hugh had an evil streak. She'd worked for him ever since she'd come to the city. First, she'd been a barely paid intern, but she'd climbed up the ladder. She'd proved herself.

And she was *not* going to get benched into doing entertainment pieces. "I'll take out the EOD reference," Gabrielle promised.

Relief slackened his features.

"But I am *not* giving this killer a name—"

Hugh waved that away. "You don't have to. I already did." He heaved down into his chair and started tapping away at his computer. "Didn't you hear me? City Stalker. No, wait, maybe D.C. Stalker—that gets it more specific, don't you think?" He snapped his fingers together. "I've got it now! The D.C. Striker!"

Her temples were pounding.

She turned away from him. There were other leads to follow. Actually, Hugh had just given her the best lead possible. She might not be able to print the story about the EOD—not yet, anyway—but now she knew where to start digging.

She just needed to get the right shovel and to dig in the right place.

There were plenty of skeletons buried in D.C. Skeletons and secrets. Time to unearth them.

"WE HAVE A PROBLEM," Cooper said, voice low, as he held his phone in a too-tight grip. "Hugh Peters knows about the EOD. He's in a closed-door meeting with Gabrielle right now, and he's telling her about us."

The line was quiet. Dead silent. "I'll take care of Peters," Mercer finally said. There was a lethal menace in the director's voice.

"What about Gabrielle?"

"Find out how much he's told her. Then we'll see if containment is necessary."

Containment? *No.* "She's just trying to help," Cooper heard himself saying. "She wants justice for the victims. She's not trying to take down the organization."

"Marshall..." Now curiosity had entered Mercer's voice. Emotion of any kind in Mercer's tone was unusual. "Just how close are you getting to the reporter?"

Not close enough.

Cooper glanced up then because he heard the sound of approaching footsteps. The curvy blonde, Penelope, was strolling toward him with a wide smile. He bit back a curse. Like he needed this now. "I'll update you ASAP." Then he ended the call. Mercer would make sure that Hugh didn't spread any more stories, and as for Gabrielle—

Over Penelope's shoulder, Cooper saw Hugh's office door open. Gabrielle stood on the threshold.

"Hello, again," Penelope said. Penelope Finn. He'd glanced down at the nameplate on her desk when he'd been trailing Gabrielle into Hugh's office.

Penelope lifted her hand toward him. "I didn't catch your name before."

Because he hadn't thrown it at her. He'd been too concentrated on Gabrielle. *And I still am.* "Cooper." Quickly, he shook her hand. Then he tried to step around her so that he could catch Gabrielle's attention.

Penelope sidestepped, keeping her body in front of his. "I was about to cut out for an early lunch. Want to join me?"

Just then, Gabrielle glanced his way. Gabrielle frowned when she saw just how close he was standing to Penelope. He was pretty sure that Gabrielle shook her head in disgust, right before she turned away and headed for the door that led to the stairwell.

"Wait!" Cooper called out.

"Oh, I'll definitely wait for you," Penelope promised him.

She couldn't be serious.

"I'm with Gabrielle," he said flatly, because that was all he needed say. "Enjoy your lunch."

Her jaw dropped, but then she gave a little laugh. "Good, *very* good response."

He didn't have the time to try to figure out that woman. He just skirted right around her. He rushed across the room and caught the stairwell door just as it was swinging closed.

He heard the clatter of Gabrielle's footsteps. Rachel had brought her a pair of high heels that morning, and it sounded like Gabrielle was trying to race away in them. He jumped down the stairs and caught her, locking his fingers around her wrist. *"Partner—"* he stressed the word "—just where are you going?"

"Digging," she mumbled. "Going to find my shovel and *dig.*"

What? He pulled her closer, positioning them into the shadows under the stairs. As far as privacy went, this place was their best bet. "I want to know what your boss told you."

She bit her lower lip.

I want to bite it.

He shoved the thought back into the darkness of his mind. Later, he could try to get that delectable mouth beneath his again. At that moment, he had to find out if the EOD agents had been compromised.

Gabrielle shook her head. "I don't want to risk you. This thing…it's bigger than I thought. If possible, even more dangerous." She tugged her arm free from him. "The partnership was a bad idea."

Oh, no. This could not happen. He held his body perfectly still. "I thought the partnership had saved your hide a few times. Your boss was the one just saying you needed a bodyguard."

"But who protects the bodyguard?" Gabrielle asked, voice sad and a little lost. "I didn't think about the risk to you. I was only concerned with myself. I can't do that anymore. I can't put you in jeopardy."

She was *protecting* him? He hadn't needed protection, not since he'd been a kid.

A scared teenager, clinging tightly to his mother's hand and begging her not to leave him. The memory flashed through his mind. There had been tears in his mother's eyes. She'd promised him, *promised,* that no matter what, she'd always be with him.

His mother had lied. Before night had fallen, she'd been gone.

He'd been alone. No father. No grandparents. *Alone.*

"I'm sorry, Cooper," Gabrielle told him. "But

this is where we end. I'll pay you for the time you helped me."

Back to payment? A growl rose in his throat.

"You can't work with me any longer. There are things that you're better off not knowing about at this point." She headed down the stairs.

He stared after her a moment. She was seriously trying to protect him, *him,* from the EOD.

Right now, he hated his job.

The secrets between them weighed heavily on his shoulders, but he knew he couldn't let things end like this.

Despite what she'd said, they weren't even *close* to an end.

He stalked after her. Just as she was about to reach for the door that would take her to the ground floor, his hand lifted, and he shoved his palm against that door, making sure she couldn't open it.

Her scent—so sweet and light, not like the cloying scent of Penelope's perfume—teased his nose.

He bent his head closer to hers, following that tempting scent. "I'm not the kind of man who gets frightened by a little danger."

"It's not little." She turned her head, met his gaze. "And I can't let you take this risk for me."

She was being honest. Brave. *Caring.* She was ripping his guts apart. He stared into her eyes, and he wanted her.

Yet the truth was that she was so far out of his league it wasn't even funny.

She deserved someone who was just as honest as she was, someone who wasn't working a second agenda.

Someone who might not have to *contain* her.

But he'd be damned if he'd step aside and let anyone else get close to her.

Cooper brushed his lips over hers. He fought to keep the kiss light, but it was a losing battle. He needed her, desperately, and he wasn't sure that he'd be able to hold back with her much longer.

Her taste drove him wild. Made him need and want—*only her.*

"Cooper..." She breathed his name.

He took that breath, drinking it from her lips. He turned her in his arms, held her close.

He wanted to give her something real. Not a lie. The desire wasn't a deception. It was as real as he could get.

She kissed him back, her response tentative at first, then stronger. Her fingers sank into his hair. Her body arched against his.

I won't give her up.

He just had to find a way to stay at her side, because there was no other place that he'd rather be.

When I'm with Gabrielle, I don't feel alone.

He felt alone when he was with other people.

Alone at the EOD. Alone on his missions, even when other teammates were with him.

He'd worked with another agent a while back, a man who seemed to have ice flowing through his veins. Drew Lancaster had been an untouchable agent. The guy had cared only about his job. No family. Few friends.

I'm just like him.

But something had changed for Drew. No, someone had changed Drew. The little doc who took care of the agents at the EOD. She'd gotten under Drew's skin and thawed his ice.

Cooper was afraid that Gabrielle was doing the same thing to him. Getting past the defenses he'd erected.

The way she made him feel could be dangerous.

He hadn't let himself care about anyone in a very, very long time. Already the force of his desire for her was so strong—

She pulled her mouth from his. He didn't let her go. His body brushed against hers.

"I won't tell you," Gabrielle said, lifting her chin, "what Hugh revealed to me in that office. So trying to seduce the information out of me just won't work."

For an instant, he saw red. His pushed her back, caging her against the wall with his body. "We need to get a few things straight," he gritted out.

Her eyes widened.

"I'm not going to be seducing you for information." Was that what the other agents at the EOD thought he was doing? "I'm kissing you and touching you…because I want you. I want you so much that I want to strip you right here and take you in this damn stairwell."

Gabrielle swallowed.

His hips were pressed against her, so she had to feel the proof of his words.

"I'm not seducing you for information—" his voice was low and hard and anger bit through each word "—I just *want you.*"

Her gaze searched his.

"And you want me," he added. "This isn't about information. It's not about anything but us."

After a brief hesitation, Gabrielle nodded.

That little nod wasn't good enough.

"You aren't going to ditch me. You're not going to make me run by saying there's danger around. Sweetheart, I've been handling danger all my life." He'd lived on the rush for years. *It's what made me feel alive.* "I can take any threat. I'm not going to run and leave you alone."

Leaving her alone was the last thing on his mind.

"I'm not running, and I *will* have you." He thought it was better to be clear about his intentions. "And when you're under me in bed, it's not going to be about seducing you for intel. It's going to be about seducing you for the sheer, hot pleasure that we can bring to each other."

Because on that point, at least, there would be no deception.

He started to step back.

Her hands flew up and curled around his shoulders. "My turn," she said, surprising him.

Cooper's brows climbed.

"I'm not seducing you so that you'll protect me from that killer out there."

She wasn't—

"When I'm with you, it's going to be because that's where I want to be. Because I *want* you." Her voice dropped, got even huskier, seemed to stroke right over his skin as she added, "And I do want you, Cooper. I want you more than I've ever wanted another man."

She was going to bring him to his knees.

"But I am *not,*" Gabrielle continued in the next instant, "going to tell you anything about the EOD. So I figure we have two choices. We can continue working as partners, but you don't get to ask me about the EOD again. You just *don't.* Hugh's afraid of the group, and if Hugh is afraid, then I am, too. I won't do anything to put you in their sights."

His teeth were clenched so tightly together that his jaw ached.

"Or we can go with option two," she said, her voice like sin. "We can forget being partners, just be lovers—and there will be no more questions asked from either of us."

His heart slammed into his chest. The blood in his veins heated and seemed to pump even faster, harder.

"There's another option," Cooper forced himself to say. "Option three. We stay partners and we become lovers." He paused, long enough to let those words sink in. "That's the option I want."

She wet her lips. "Me, too..."

Then that was the option they would take. And, maybe...maybe Gabrielle never had to learn the truth about him. If he could keep her away from the EOD, then Gabrielle could keep believing he was just a P.I. who lived in her brownstone.

They could keep being partners...and lovers.

He backed away from her. *For now.* She skirted toward the door and stepped into the lobby. But then she paused. Her hand reached for his. Her fingers curled around his.

The touch was so innocent and light. An ache grew in his chest. "Gabrielle," he began, but then Cooper saw the man rushing toward him. The man with a badge clipped on his belt and a burning glare on his face.

Detective Carmichael had just joined the party.

"Lane?" Gabrielle didn't release Cooper's hand. "Do you have news? Did you find out about—"

The detective braked to a hard stop right in front of her. "Why didn't you call me?" He *pulled* Gabrielle away from Cooper. "I just heard about the break-in! Damn it, Gabby, you should have let me know right away! I would have rushed over!"

And Cooper realized that all along, the detective had responded a little too personally to Gabrielle.

I've had one lover.

Jealousy thickened within Cooper. He had the feeling he was looking at Gabrielle's ex. He should have seen it before.

"You're homicide," Gabrielle said as she glanced around the lobby. They'd attracted a few stares. "This was a B&E. Cooper said he had friends who could help and they—"

Carmichael sent a withering glare Cooper's way. "I'm sure he has plenty of *friends.* Just like the friend who managed to get him hauled out of my precinct last night."

Cooper gave him a grim smile. *Get your hands off her, cop.*

Carmichael maneuvered Gabrielle to the right, getting them in a private corner. Cooper followed right with him.

"You and I are both connecting the dots, Gabby," Carmichael said.

Cooper hated the way the other man said *Gabby*. Her name was Gabrielle. A beautiful name for a beautiful woman.

"It's no simple B&E. You know it. The guy is after you." He rolled back his shoulders and finally let her go. "I want you to consider moving into a safe house."

"No." Her immediate response. "I have my own guard—my partner." Her gaze darted to Cooper. "I'm safer with him than I'd be anywhere else."

"With *anyone* else," Cooper clarified. Because the cop wasn't going to keep Gabrielle safe. Cooper was.

You're an ex for a reason, buddy.

Cooper was suddenly determined to find out that reason.

"What do you really know about him?" Carmichael demanded as he rounded to glare at Cooper. "Because I've been digging into your past, Marshall."

Cooper stared levelly back at the man. Was he supposed to be worried? He knew that his service records were shielded, courtesy of the EOD.

"You were in a boarding school until you were eighteen. Then…somehow…even though your mother was dead and you had no other relatives, you got a paid ride from an unknown benefactor. Four years at Yale."

The detective *had* been digging. But he still hadn't discovered anything particularly impressive.

"Four years, then you vanished. Not a blip on the radar until a year ago when you came back to D.C. and started working as a P.I."

He hadn't vanished. He'd enlisted. And unless Carmichael got a whole lot more authorization, he wouldn't ever see Cooper's records. Cooper exhaled slowly. Carmichael was an annoyance, nothing more. "Perhaps you should spend less time looking into my past and a little more time looking for the killer. The city would be safer then."

Carmichael lunged toward him.

Gabrielle put herself between Cooper and the detective. Carmichael kept glaring. In turn, Cooper kept his faint smile in place.

The smile hid the fact that *I'm really starting to hate that cop.*

"Cooper isn't a threat to me. He and I are the ones that are giving you leads, so you need to back off," Gabrielle's voice was fierce.

Carmichael didn't look like he was ready to back anyplace.

"I don't think you should trust him," Carmichael muttered.

"I do, though. Because he's had my back every step of the way."

No, he hadn't. Shame twisted with the jealousy inside of him.

"And speaking of leads…" Gabrielle said as she pushed back her hair. "We have to follow one now." She put her hand on Cooper's arm, but her stare was on the cop's face. "If we find out anything you can use, I'll contact you. Just like always—*before* I put anything in the paper."

So that was part of their relationship. Carmichael had been busting lots of perps in the past six months, earning commendations…with Gabrielle's help?

"I've got my phone on me," she added. "You can call me if you need to reach me, Lane."

The detective leaned toward her. "And if you need me, anytime or anyplace, you call. Don't let me find out about a break-in the next day, got it? I…care about you. Remember that."

Then he was gone, storming toward the lobby's doors.

Cooper didn't move. Emotion had been thick in the cop's voice.

"I really do have a lead for us to follow," Gabrielle said, sighing. "That wasn't just me trying to get rid of him."

He turned his head. Found her eyes on him. "You were the one to break things off."

Gabrielle winced. "You think you figured us out. Just after that little chat?"

He thought he wanted to know everything

about the cop right then. Carmichael had torn into his past—turnabout would only be fair.

"No, not yet." He would though.

For now, he took her hand, threaded his fingers through hers. Even though his hand was so much bigger than hers, they seemed to fit. "So… where's this lead?"

She gave him a half smile. "Hope you don't mind a little trip to jail. Because that's exactly where we're headed."

Chapter Seven

She was burning through her favors at an insanely fast rate.

Gabrielle walked through the Department of Corrections, her heels clicking lightly on the floor. She'd had to use two favors just to get in the DOC—and to get access to Johnny Zacks.

Johnny was awaiting sentencing for a heist he'd done a month ago. Another jewelry store break-in, his fourth. Only this time, Johnny had gotten shot by a security guard.

Johnny Zacks had been breaking into jewelry stores for the last few months. He was usually in and out without a trace.

Except for this time…

Johnny was already waiting in the room for her. He was cuffed to the table, and a bored-looking guard stood in the corner, watching him.

"Thanks, Quent," Gabrielle said to the guard. He'd been the one to first connect her to Johnny.

Quent might look like he didn't give a damn, but he did. The man had a giant heart.

Quent's head barely inclined at her words.

Johnny, young, tan, with blond hair that was too long and wide blue eyes, glanced suspiciously at Cooper. "Who's the muscle?"

"My partner." Saying that was getting easier and easier. "He's helping me to look for your sister's killer."

She felt, more than saw, Cooper's surprise.

"Y-you've got news on Kylie?" Johnny asked.

Johnny was actually Kylie's half brother. He'd been out of the country when she was killed, and when he'd come back and discovered that his sister had been murdered, the guy had broken apart.

And gone on a robbery spree.

It seemed that Johnny was the wild child in the family. Kylie had been his strength. Without her, he was still floundering.

"I believe that the man who killed your sister has taken three more lives."

Johnny's hands fisted.

"He's still in the city, the cops are looking for him now—"

"Because more people are dead." Disgust tightened Johnny's face. "They should've been looking for him before! They shouldn't have given up on Kylie!"

"I'm not giving up on her," Gabrielle said softly. "You know that. I gave you my word."

Johnny sucked in a ragged breath and nodded.

"I need to ask you a few more questions about your sister's boyfriend—"

"Fiancé," Johnny cut in, straightening. "They were getting married. She called me and told me that she was marrying Keith. She was so excited." His voice softened. "That was the last time I talked with her. I try to remember her that way, happy, you know?"

"I know," she told him, her heart aching.

Cooper pulled up a chair and sat down next to her at the table.

Gabrielle cleared her throat. "Johnny, you told me that you met Keith a few times. Was there… anything about the guy that set off alarms for you?"

"Alarms?" His head cocked and his face scrunched.

Wait, wrong word. Treading more carefully, Gabrielle said, "It's hard for me to find a lot of information on him. He's—"

"He was ex-military," Johnny said at once, then he jerked his head toward Cooper. "Like him."

Her body tensed. "How do you know that?" She hadn't found any enlistment records for Keith Lockwood.

Johnny smiled. When he smiled, he looked

even younger than his twenty-two years. "I can always spot 'em. Me and Kylie, we grew up bouncing around military bases. Our dad commanded one…'til he died." His shoulders rolled back. "It's in the walk. The posture." He tapped his temple. "I can always tell." He pointed at Cooper. "I pegged you the minute you walked in."

Cooper didn't respond.

"Did Lockwood *say* he was in the military?" Gabrielle pressed. She didn't want to tell Johnny that she doubted his word, but—

"Kylie told me," he replied. "Her guy would have nightmares. Maybe flashbacks, I don't know what they were exactly. He'd wake up, screaming about his team, about someone getting left behind."

Excitement had her hands trembling. "Did your sister ever mention if Lockwood worked for a specific unit?"

Johnny shook his head. "It was some kind of black ops deal, I know that much. Kylie told me that whenever she asked Keith about it, he said he *couldn't* tell her, and that man…hell, he usually told her everything. But he was walking away. They were going to start fresh." He blinked and seemed to see the past. "Kylie was happy. Did I tell you that? When she called me, she was happy."

Gabrielle swallowed the knot in her throat. "You did."

He nodded. "Kylie liked pretty things. Things that sparkled." His dimples flashed again. "I gave Kylie pretty things. She needed them, you know? I wanted her to go to heaven with them. So she'd sparkle up there—"

"Johnny." She said his name deliberately, to bring him back. The grief still got to him. Still hurt him. "I am going to find her killer. I told you I wouldn't give up, and I won't."

His head bowed. "Thank you."

"But you have to keep your promise, too, remember?"

Cooper was watching them, so quiet and intense.

"You take the plea deal, you get some counseling and you don't ever steal again."

He looked up at her. "I don't need to steal. I gave Kylie what she wanted." His eyes narrowed. "And you'll give her what she needs. Justice."

"I will."

A buzzer sounded then, and Quent stepped forward. "I've got to take Johnny back now."

"Thank you." Gabrielle rose. There were more questions she wanted to ask, but Johnny had already confirmed her growing suspicions.

She didn't speak again until Johnny and Quent were gone. Then she focused on Cooper. She started to tell him about her new theory, but then she hesitated. "Was he right?" Gabrielle found herself asking instead. "Are you ex-military?"

Emotion vanished from his eyes. Strange, she could actually see the mask slipping into place. Why hadn't she noticed that before?

Just when she thought he wasn't going to answer her, Cooper said, "I was."

"Those missing years," she murmured. "The years Carmichael couldn't find in your past. You were on active duty."

He inclined his head. "Guilty."

"What branch?"

"I joined the Air Force." There was a brief pause, then, "I was a PJ—a pararescue jumper."

Her eyes widened. "You jumped out of the planes." It wasn't the jumping out that was the danger—it was what he jumped *into* that could be so terrifying.

"I did my job," Cooper said simply.

Talk about a major understatement. She'd read reports on PJs before. Those guys jumped into infernos, into war zones and even into the paths of hurricanes.

She rocked back on her heels. "No wonder you were used to the adrenaline rushes."

"Told you," he said as his eyes glinted, "I've got plenty of experience with them."

"Why'd you give it up?" Gabrielle asked him. "What made you turn away from that life?"

"Because I got a better offer." He shrugged, as if the change didn't matter. "I get to make my rules now, and I'm still helping people."

She smiled at him. "Yes, you are." She headed for the door. "Johnny gave us a real lead in there." They cleared the guard areas and headed back outside. "I already know that Van McAdams was in the military."

"How are you so sure?"

The sun glared down on them in the parking lot as they paused near his motorcycle.

"The killer sliced his neck open." She pulled in a deep breath. "And he sliced through the dog tags that were around Van's throat. I saw the dog tags in the blood near him." She gave a firm nod. "That's two men dead, both men who were in the military—"

"Plenty of people were in the military." He didn't seem to be jumping on board with her idea.

Maybe he needed more of a push. Shading her eyes, she told him, "I want to find out what, where and when they served. If Lockwood and McAdams were together, if they knew each other… *that* could lead us to the killer."

Thunder rumbled in the distance. A storm would be hitting that night. But that still left them with plenty of time to follow up on more leads.

"We're getting closer," Gabrielle whispered. "I can feel it. I—" She broke off when her phone began to ring. Gabrielle yanked it out of her bag and she frowned when she saw *Blocked* on the caller ID.

"Is it Carmichael?" Cooper asked as he pressed closer. "Has he found something new?"

She swiped her finger across the screen so she could take the call. "Harper," she said.

"He's not who you think..." The voice was low, rasping, and she had to strain to hear the words.

Gabrielle put her hand over her left ear, trying to drown out the noise from the lot and the street as she focused on the call. "I can't hear you—say that again."

"Cooper Marshall isn't who you think..." The voice was still low, still rasping, as if the caller were trying to disguise his voice.

But this time, she clearly understood his words. Her gaze flew to Cooper. He frowned back at her.

"He's right there, in front of you, and he's lying to you." A rough laugh. "Lying right to your face."

Her stare slid away from Cooper and she scanned the lot. "You're watching me."

More laughter. "You interest me. You shouldn't have even been in the game, yet here you are, leading the race."

"I didn't realize we were playing a game." There was no accent to his voice, at least, not one that she could detect.

"Of course, winner kills all—"

Fear had her voice cracking as she said, "People's lives aren't part of a game!" Then she mouthed *It's him* to Cooper.

Cooper immediately tried to reach for the phone, but she backed away from him.

"Good, good," the voice in her ear praised her. "Don't let him get too close. That's what he's trying to do. Get close to you. Lie to you. Use you."

Like she was going to believe a killer.

"He's not who you think…don't trust the wrong man. Doing that will just get you killed."

Then the line went dead.

For a moment, she didn't move at all. *Where is he?*

"Gabrielle?" Cooper touched her arm.

She flinched. "He's here. He's watching us." She spun around, her gaze searching all around the area.

Cooper took the phone from her. He tried to do a call return.

"You can't," she said, her eyes still scanning the area. "He blocked the call."

Cooper pulled her back toward the shelter of the building. Cars were in front of them. The heavy stone of the building behind them. As far as protection went, it sure seemed like a good spot to her.

Cooper put his phone to his ear. A few seconds later, he said, "Rachel, the SOB just called Gabrielle. See if…if Sydney," he said as his gaze fell away from Gabrielle's, "can hack into the system and find him."

She figured Sydney must be another one of his useful friends. Those friends were sure coming in handy.

"She says that he's watching us," Cooper continued. "We're at the DOC. Yeah, yeah, I want a search."

A search for the killer sounded like an excellent plan to her.

"I'm going now. I'm sending Gabrielle back in with the guards."

Whoa, he was benching her?

He ended the call and secured the phone back in his pocket. His stare leveled on her. "Get inside. Stay there until I come for you."

"While you face him alone?" That sounded like a horrible plan.

His smile was grim. "You don't need to worry about me. I've got this."

He was cold and deadly and he didn't show even a hint of fear.

He's not who you think.

"Get inside," Cooper ordered her.

Now she knew why he seemed to be so good at giving orders. That was the military in him, coming out.

Only she wasn't so good at following orders. Especially in a *partnership.* "I'll call Carmichael."

His jaw hardened. "Do what you need to do."

Uh, calling the cops *counted* as doing what she needed to do.

"I have to know that you're safe, Gabrielle, or I can't look for him. Every minute we waste…he could be getting away."

She managed a nod, but she sure wasn't happy about him racing out alone. Then she was inside and he just—gone in an instant. She glanced around, looking through the window, but she could find no trace of him.

A chill settled over her as she kept staring outside.

Don't trust the wrong man. Doing that will just get you killed.

She didn't plan on dying.

"THE KILLER JUST made contact with Gabrielle Harper," Bruce Mercer said as he lowered the phone back onto his desk. His gaze lifted and locked on Noelle Evers.

The FBI profiler had arrived less than an hour ago. She'd come right to him so that he could begin briefing her on the hell they faced.

Outsiders didn't normally get this close to the EOD. Noelle Evers had passed one very thorough background check in order to get her insider access.

But he trusted Noelle—mostly because he knew her secrets.

Behind her glasses, Noelle's eyes widened. She'd pulled the glasses out a few moments before to begin reading the files that he'd gathered for her.

"That's a very dangerous sign," she said.

He didn't need to be told that.

"But...that's also something we can use," Noelle continued. "If the reporter can draw the killer out, then the authorities will have a better chance of catching him—"

"The local cops aren't catching him. The EOD is containing him."

Her head cocked. "He *is* the EOD." Her fingers curled around the files in her lap. Files on Lockwood and McAdams. And on the other two agents who'd been killed—Frank Malone and Jessica Flintwood. "These agents were highly trained. They could kill in an instant, yet they never had the chance to fight back against their attacker. He's a man they trust implicitly." She squared her shoulders. "I know you told me that my access would be limited, but I need to see the files of every agent they worked with on their missions."

He was already shaking his head before she finished speaking.

Her delicate jaw hardened even as her hazel eyes narrowed on him. "Lockwood and McAdams let the killer in because they trusted him. You trust a man or a woman who has protected your back in the field. They let him in, just as Malone and Flintwood did."

"I can't give you access to the files of existing agents."

"You are tying my hands!"

He rose. "Then find a way to untie them. You're here to work up the profile so that I can see which of my agents might best fit it. You can build the profile without digging into confidential records."

Noelle rose, too. She was a tall woman, skirting close to five foot nine, and she had on high heels that gave her an additional two inches. "If I can't talk to the agents, what about the reporter?"

He smiled. "Of course, but don't let her know about us."

"Of course," she muttered right back.

Mercer headed for the door. Noelle wasn't the only one who wanted to question that reporter. He needed to find out exactly what the rogue had said to her.

"He may have made similar contact with the other victims," Noelle said, her words making him pause near the door.

Mercer glanced back at her.

"I figure we have two options with him. Either

this is part of his MO—he calls his victims, he taunts them, and then he kills them…"

Mercer waited.

"Or else he's contacting Gabrielle Harper *because* she's a reporter. He wants the attention that she can give him."

"He wants to expose the EOD."

Noelle nodded. The light glinted off the lenses of her glasses. "He's killing agents—"

"*Punishing* the EOD," Mercer said. He'd done his share of profiling over the years, too.

"So why not take it one step further? Show the world just how dangerous the EOD truly is."

That couldn't happen. Too many lives were on the line.

"I'll arrange a meeting between you and the reporter." He just had to pull a few strings.

Then they had to figure out…was Gabrielle Harper becoming the killer's target? Or did the rogue think she could be another weapon to use against the EOD?

THE SOB HAD actually *called* her. Rage still beat in Cooper's blood. Hours had passed since that phone call. He'd searched the area near the DOC but had found no trace of the killer.

He'd taken Gabrielle back to the brownstone. The cops had finally cleared out, but Gabrielle hadn't shown any interest in going upstairs to her place.

She'd gone straight for his apartment instead.

The storm that had been threatening all day had finally erupted. He heard the clatter of thunder as the pelting drops of rain fell outside.

Gabrielle was on his couch. She'd kicked off her shoes and tucked her feet under her body. She looked small—delicate.

And scared.

Her fear pissed him off.

He stalked toward her. His knees brushed the couch. "He's not going to hurt you."

She looked up at him. He hadn't been able to hear the caller's words, not clearly, and he hadn't wanted to push her for more information with so many eyes and ears around. She'd talked with Carmichael about the call, but the cop had pulled her away from Cooper for that little chat.

He forced his jaw to unlock as he stared down at her. "I need to know what he said."

Because Mercer had already called him—twice—demanding details.

"He...he told me that you weren't who I thought you were." Her arms wrapped around her stomach. "He told me that you were lying to me."

His heartbeat seemed to echo in his ears.

"He knew your name," she continued without

looking away from him. "And he told me that you weren't who I thought."

Bastard. "He's trying to shake you up. To make you afraid."

"I *am* afraid."

"Don't stop trusting me." He reached down, caught her hands and pulled her up so that she stood beside him. "He wants you to turn away from me so that you'll be on your own, vulnerable."

I won't have that. The rogue wasn't going to take Gabrielle's life. Cooper didn't plan to walk into an apartment and smell her blood.

Or find her lying on the floor, motionless.

"Cooper?" Gabrielle frowned at him. "Are you all right?"

No, he wasn't. His heart wasn't drumming in his ears any longer. It didn't seem to be beating at all. His body felt cold, like ice that sank through skin and bone. "I won't do it."

Her head tilted toward him. Her dark hair slid over her shoulder. The move exposed the golden column of her neck.

Sliced open, bleeding out...

"Do what?" Gabrielle asked him as she searched his gaze.

"I won't find you dead. It's not happening." He knew what the cold was in that instant—fear.

Fear didn't burn, it chilled, and it was freezing him from the inside, out.

He pulled Gabrielle close and put his mouth against hers.

The rogue couldn't get her. The killer wasn't going to drive a wedge between Cooper and Gabrielle, and the guy *wasn't* going to kill her.

The kiss was hard, too rough. But Cooper wasn't in control then. The ice had to melt. He had to get closer to Gabrielle, had to make sure that she was safe.

His hands wrapped around her body. Her mouth was open, so sweet and hot. He drove his tongue past her lips and tasted.

Took.

He lifted her into his arms.

There would be no stopping this time. He couldn't.

Cooper carried her back to the bedroom, kissing her the entire time.

Desire pulsed within him, growing stronger with every step, tangling with the fear and the fury within him.

Lightning flashed. Thunder shook the windowpanes.

He lowered her to her feet, letting her bare toes skim the hardwood, positioning her near the edge of the bed. Light from the lamp spilled over the bed.

Cooper stepped back from her. He couldn't give her honesty about all parts of his life, but in this moment, he would give her everything that he could.

"I want you." His voice was gravel rough with desire. "Trust that. Trust *me*."

Her gaze held his. He could see her need shining in her gaze. "I do," she said softly.

That broke him. The last of his control vanished.

She started to lift up the edge of her shirt. His fingers caught hers. He wound up throwing that shirt across the room.

His hands stroked her, caressed. Her skin was softer than silk, smooth and perfect.

She wore a black, lacy bra. A temptation that was going to force him to his knees.

But then her hand went to her jeans. She shimmied out of her jeans. Long, tan legs were bared to him. Those legs—and the matching scrap of black lace panties that covered her hips.

Don't pounce. Because he wanted to pounce. He wanted to take and take and take and let the pleasure drive out the last of the chill that clung to his skin.

Instead, he lowered her onto the bed. He kissed. He touched. Her bra joined her clothes when he tossed it to the floor. Her breasts were perfect, full with tight, pink tips. His tongue licked those taut peaks. She arched against him. Her nails dug into his back, pressing through the thin T-shirt that he wore.

Her hips pushed up against him. Her spread legs moved restlessly against his body.

His hands slid down to the front of her panties. Panties that had surely been designed to make a man go crazy. Carefully, he stroked her through the lace. She was hot and so ready for him.

He had to make this good for her. He wanted Gabrielle as wild and hungry as he was.

His fingers pushed into her. Her breath rushed out.

Then she was the one yanking up his T-shirt and trying to touch his skin.

But when she touched him…

I need her too much.

He pulled back and stripped in seconds. He reached into the nightstand and fumbled for the protection he'd put there.

Then he slowly removed the scrap of lace that covered her sex. He tried to be careful, but he wanted her so badly—the lace ripped.

Gabrielle just laughed. She lifted her hips toward him. "I don't want to wait anymore."

Her voice—her husky words—pushed him over the edge. His hands closed over her thighs. He parted them even more, making room for his body. He put his aroused flesh against her.

Their gazes locked.

He drove into her with one long, hard thrust.

Her breath gasped out. Her eyes darkened even more. Cooper stilled, worried that he was hurting her.

At his hesitation, her legs wrapped around his hips. She arched against him. "More," Gabrielle whispered.

He'd give her more. He'd give her all that he had.

His fingers threaded with hers. He withdrew then thrust harder, deeper, again and again. The moans she made urged him on. They were the sexiest sounds he'd ever heard. Pleasure waited, so close, so close. Her body felt amazing against his. Being *in* her, that hot, tight paradise of her body—it made the blood in his body seem to burn.

She cried out and he saw the pleasure on her face. Her cheeks flushed. Her eyes went blind.

She whispered his name.

He drove into her, not able to hold back. The headboard thudded into the wall, and when the pleasure hit him, it was like nothing he'd felt before.

His body shuddered as he pumped into her. He held her with hands that were too tight, but he couldn't let go.

She was all he knew. The only thing he wanted.

The one thing that he wasn't going to give up.

His gaze met hers. Pleasure was a drug making him desperate, light-headed.

Gabrielle smiled up at him.

For Cooper, in that instant, *everything* changed.

THE RAIN FELL down in a hard, heavy torrent. The local forecasters had predicted that the storm would last for hours.

Cooper had taken the reporter home.

He'd called, given Gabrielle a warning that she should heed, but the woman had seemed to pay him no attention.

Her mistake.

She would learn the truth soon enough.

When you trusted the wrong person, you wound up dead.

Another woman had trusted Cooper once. She'd believed in him, just as Gabrielle believed in the man now.

That woman was buried in a cemetery thirty miles away.

Soon, Cooper would be buried, too.

The killer pulled up his coat and whistled as he turned away from the brownstone.

It was almost time for his next attack. Almost…

Chapter Eight

He didn't look nearly as fierce when he slept. Gabrielle turned her head, letting her gaze slide over Cooper's face. The danger was gone. The dark intensity vanished when he was unaware.

He looked younger but still as handsome.

Just not as deadly.

His blond hair was mussed. The brilliant blue of his eyes was hidden. His tanned skin looked even darker against the white of the sheets.

And, in the light, Gabrielle could see that Cooper had scars—a lot of them.

When they'd made love, her fingers had skimmed over his body. She'd been so far gone, though, that she hadn't recognized the rough outline of the scars for what they were.

Her stare drifted down his body. Since the sheet pooled at his hips, she had a great view of his truly impressive chest and abs.

And the seven scars there. She counted those scars again. Yes. Seven.

From gunshots? Knife wounds? Just what had happened to Cooper in his life? What made him so dangerous?

He's not who you think he is.

That dark voice wouldn't get out of her head.

She couldn't escape into sleep, not the way Cooper could. Maybe it was the storm. Storms always reminded her too much of her past.

It had been storming—a fierce, hard storm, just like this one—the night she'd found her father.

The thunder had cloaked the sound of the gunshot. None of her neighbors had even known that he was hurt.

By the time she'd gotten home, it had been too late.

Lightning flashed outside of the window.

Swallowing, Gabrielle lifted her hand. One of Cooper's arms had curled over her stomach. Carefully, she eased out from under that arm. Then she put his hand back down on the bed. Her gaze studied his face closely, but he didn't stir.

She pulled on his robe. It was there, so surely he wouldn't mind if she borrowed it, right?

Gabrielle tiptoed out of his bedroom. It was still early, barely past nine at night, and there was no way she could sleep.

Once back in the den, she hesitated.

The place just seemed so empty. Why didn't

Cooper have any personal mementos there? His place…it was just like Van McAdams's.

Van and Keith had been in the military, and so had Cooper.

She glanced over her shoulder.

Why had Cooper been at the scene of Keith Lockwood's death that first night? She'd thought it was just coincidence at the time, but…

She found herself creeping toward the small desk in the corner. A laptop sat on the desk, closed, turned off. Her fingers slid over the laptop.

She'd just made love with a man—and she knew only the barest of details about his past.

Gabrielle leaned down. There were two drawers on the side of the desk. Neither showed signs of having a lock.

"What are you doing?"

Cooper's voice came from *right* behind her. She jumped, spun around then tried to suck in a deep gulp of air. "Cooper, you just scared five years of my life away!"

She hadn't even heard him approach. He'd snuck up on her the same way he had at Lockwood's apartment.

His eyes were narrowed as they raked her face. "You left me."

"I couldn't sleep." Thanks to that little scare, her heart raced in her chest. "I thought I'd get up and—"

"You were going into my desk."

What was up with his accusing tone? Talk about going from sensual to suspicion in sixty seconds flat. Her hands tightened on the robe. "No, I wasn't. I wouldn't do that to you." The accusation was an insult. "Look, just because I'm a reporter, it doesn't mean I snoop on my friends—"

His eyelids flickered. "Is that what we are?" His head tilted. "Because I thought we were lovers now."

He wore a pair of jeans that hung low on his hips. A line of stubble lined his jaw. He looked rough, tough and sexy.

Gabrielle wet her too-dry lips. "I think we can be both." She found herself leaning toward him, so she snapped her shoulders back. "But we need to be clear. You said I can trust you, and I want you to trust me, too."

He glanced away from her.

What was that about?

Gabrielle took a bracing breath and plowed on. "I want to know you. Who you were before you came to D.C. Who you are now." Because she didn't want her lover to be a stranger to her.

Thunder rumbled again. She flinched.

His brows pulled low. "Why does the storm scare you? I thought nothing scared you."

Gabrielle laughed at that. "You're so wrong. I'm just usually better at hiding my fear." His shoulders seemed so wide. He was strong and solid standing there, and he made her feel like she didn't need to fear.

He made her feel safe so perhaps that was why her words just kept flowing. "I found him during a storm like this one."

"Him?"

"My father. He was waiting for me at home. I was out late, at a football game with some friends. I came home sure he was going to get all over me for breaking curfew…" Gabrielle glanced toward the window. "But when I went in, our house was dead silent. Silent and so dark. My dad always left the light on for me. He'd sit in his chair and he'd watch TV until I came home." Her gaze drifted back to him.

Cooper didn't touch her. He just watched her as lightning lit up the room once more.

If she wanted to know about his past, it only seemed fair that she should reveal hers to him.

"He wasn't in his chair. He was on the floor lying on his back. I ran to him, I begged him to talk to me, but he was gone."

Her father's eyes had been so empty. As empty as Van McAdams's. The life had been completely gone from his stare. She'd never forget the sight of his empty gaze.

"What happened to him?"

"He was shot. One bullet, right in the heart."

Her own heart hurt every time she remembered that night.

"I'm sorry." His arms reached for her. Cooper pulled her against his chest. At his touch, tears welled in her eyes. It had been over eight years, but she still missed her father.

He'd been her constant. Her hero.

Her mother had cut out on them when Gabrielle had just been a toddler. Run away with a married man and never looked back.

"The police said it was a robbery gone wrong. Some cash and electronics were taken, but..." She squeezed her eyes shut and pulled in a steadying breath when the thunder rolled once more. "But they never found the person who killed him. The trail went cold, and he was forgotten." Gabrielle forced herself to pull back so that she could gaze up into Cooper's eyes.

"That's why you do it," he said softly.

"That's why," she agreed. She'd never been able to give her father justice, and that knowledge ate away at her. "I give the other families what I can't get."

He shook his head. "You're not what I thought..."

His words made her stiffen. They were too similar to the killer's. "You're *exactly* what—who—I thought you were," she fired back fiercely. "You've had my back. You've risked your life. You—"

He kissed her.

You're one hell of a kisser. Because she'd thought he would be, from the first glimpse that she'd had of him. She'd almost dropped her chocolate chip cookies because she'd taken one look and gotten lost in his blue gaze.

His lips were firm and warm, and the things that man could do with his tongue…

Cooper eased away from her. "I'd risk my life for you in an instant. Know that. I'll protect you with every bit of power I have."

She believed him.

"Sometimes, I think all our pasts can do is hurt us." His words were a rumble. His right hand curled under her jaw. "It's the future that I like to think about. What can be."

But a past couldn't be forgotten, or completely buried, no matter how much you might wish it to be so.

Why wasn't Cooper telling her about himself?

She felt as if she'd just laid her soul bare for him.

Goose bumps rose on her skin. She backed away from him, hunching her shoulders a bit. When lightning flashed again, Gabrielle didn't flinch, and she was rather proud of that fact.

But she was also curious. About Cooper. Always—him. "What scares you?" Gabrielle whispered.

He didn't move. No, he did. A small movement. He *tensed.* "What makes you think anything does?"

Her lips lifted in a wan smile. "Everyone fears something. Even you, tough guy." Even the man who jumped into fires.

His eyes were on her, burning bright. "Maybe *you* scare me."

His response surprised her. "Why?"

A phone rang then, vibrating from its position on the couch. Cooper's lips thinned, but then he said, "Because I don't want you hurt."

Her lips parted in surprise, but he had already reached for the phone. He answered it, even as his eyes stayed on her. "Marshall." His eyelids flickered a bit. "Yes, she's here."

The call was about her?

He turned away from Gabrielle, showing her his broad back. "We're not coming out in the storm. Why? Because she doesn't like damn storms, that's why."

Her breath caught in her throat.

"When it's over, *that's* when we can talk," Cooper growled.

Another phone rang then—her phone. She instantly recognized the familiar beat of music that alerted her to the caller's identity. Gabrielle hurried across the room, vaguely aware that Cooper had ended his call and followed her.

Her fingers trembled a bit as she picked up her phone. She took the call saying, "Penelope, look, this isn't a good time for me—"

"Something is happening here," Penelope whispered.

"What?"

"After you left a man and a woman in suits—you know, the boring, government-type suits—came in to the *Inquisitor.* They went into Hugh's office. They closed the door, and now Hugh is about to leave town for a trip down to the Cayman Islands."

What? Hugh was heading off to the islands? That made zero sense to her.

"Get in here!" Penelope ordered.

Then the woman hung up on her.

After her day, Gabrielle really didn't need Penelope's drama.

Gabrielle hurriedly tried getting her boss on the line. Only he wasn't picking up. The guy *never* ignored a call from any of his reporters. And Hugh also didn't just rush out of town. In fact, he usually stayed at the *Inquisitor* until after midnight most nights.

What's going on?

She looked up. Cooper had his eyes on her. "My boss is leaving town." She rubbed the growing knot of tension in the back of her neck. "Some strange folks in suits came in, and Penelope was pretty much saying they've pressured him to leave." *Government-type suits.* "Feds," she muttered.

Cooper's brows climbed. "Uh, you think Feds are pressuring your boss to get out of D.C.?"

Her gaze cut to the window. "I have to get down to the *Inquisitor*."

"You just told me that you don't like storms."

"No, I don't," she agreed quickly. "They scare the ever-loving hell out of me. But I can't let fear stop me." She never had, never would.

She headed for the bedroom.

He blocked her path. "Maybe *we* should get out of town."

Her eyes widened. "What?" But, before he could reply, Gabrielle shook her head. "I can't! I have a story, people counting on me—"

"You have a killer calling you, threatening you. You need to get out of sight and get some place safe." He gave a hard nod. "I can keep you safe. I can take you someplace that no one else would ever be able to find."

His words held an ominous ring that unsettled her. "I don't want to vanish. I'm not hiding." She brushed past him.

"Fine." That word was bitten off. "I'll take you to the *Inquisitor*."

Gabrielle stopped at the bedroom door and swung back to face him. "Uh, try that again."

She motioned to the window. "I'm not getting on your motorcycle. We'll take a cab. My whole facing-your-fears bit only goes so far."

For an instant, she thought he'd smile at her.

But then he did that little trick of his—that trick where all emotion vanished from his face and eyes. "When you want to vanish, tell me. Remember that, okay? I can get you out of this game anytime."

"It's not a game."

"Isn't it?"

Life and death shouldn't be a game.

And Cooper's words shouldn't have reminded her of the killer.

But they did.

The killer's voice seemed to echo in her mind.

"Winner kills all."

HUGH'S COMPUTER WAS gone. His files were boxed up.

And he was sweating.

Gabrielle stood in the doorway of his office, frowning. "Hugh?"

His head jerked up at her call.

"What happened here?"

He cleared his throat and gave a shrug. "Vacation time," he told her with a too-jovial tone in his voice. "Got some coming, so I thought I'd head out for a few days."

Bull. She glanced at Cooper. He shrugged. Raindrops clung to the sides of his hair.

Gabrielle marched into Hugh's office. "Come in and shut the door, Cooper." Because this conversation wasn't going further than the three of them.

She slapped her hands against the surface of Hugh's desk. His Adam's apple bobbed as he watched her.

"You don't run from anything," she told him. "And you taught me not to run."

"I'm not running." That false jovial air weakened. "It's a vacation, I told you that."

The door clicked shut.

"Who got to you? Did the cops put pressure on you because of that call I—"

He reached across the desk and grabbed her left hand. "You're in too deep."

Gabrielle shook her head. "I'm a reporter. You taught me that there can *never* be a 'too deep'—this is our job. To follow the truth, no matter where it might take us."

"What if it takes you to the grave?"

"Hugh..."

He freed her and rolled his shoulders. "Feds confiscated my computer. They told me they believed that the killer had hacked into the system here at the *Inquisitor*, that he'd been using my own intel to get close to you. That was how he knew where you lived, knew your phone number… The Feds said they traced him, they found evidence he'd been in your personnel file. Every bit of info I had on you…" He paused and his chin lifted. "The killer's got it now, too."

"How do they know that?" she demanded. "They can't know! They—"

"Were they just trying to come up with a reason to take my computer? My files? Maybe," Hugh allowed, "but they had a court order, so it wasn't like I could stop them from taking everything."

Cooper, standing just behind her, remained silent.

"Why the trip out of town?" Gabrielle asked.

Hugh's gaze slid away from hers. "I've made a lot of enemies with my stories over the years."

"And you never ran from any of those enemies."

His head inclined. "But I'd leave in an instant if it meant I could keep my people safe."

He's leaving for me. The knowledge was twisting her insides into knots. "What did they tell you?" Gabrielle demanded.

Hugh reached for his bag. His attention shifted to Cooper. "Should have realized it sooner," Hugh mumbled. "But maybe it's a good thing that you're here."

Her blood iced. *No, no, no.*

Hugh's smile stretched across his face. She knew that smile. It was his fake smile. One he gave when he was in the presence of an enemy.

She wasn't Hugh's enemy. That just left…Cooper.

"If anyone can keep her safe, I guess it will be you, bodyguard." Hugh walked around the desk, clutching his bag. He paused for just a moment beside Gabrielle. "I'll be seeing you again. You can count on it."

Her heart felt like it was about to burst from her chest.

Hugh didn't trust Cooper. She sure got the message he'd sent her—loud and clear—*should have realized it sooner.*

Hugh reached for her. He hugged her—and slipped a small flash drive into her hand.

Her fingers curled around the drive, concealing it completely.

He pulled away. This time his smile was real. It reached his eyes. "You know I can't turn away from a good story," he said.

No, he couldn't.

"I'll be back."

He strode toward the door. Cooper started to slide out of his path, but Hugh stopped him. Hugh slapped a hand down on Cooper's shoulder. "If Gabrielle gets so much as a bruise…"

Gabrielle slipped the flash drive into her back pocket.

"…you'll answer to me."

Then Hugh was gone.

Cooper glanced her way. "What the hell was that about?"

It was about Hugh not trusting him. About Hugh being forced out of D.C., but by whom?

Her money was on the EOD. She needed to access that flash drive, but Hugh had concealed it from Cooper for a reason, and she didn't want his eyes on it, not until she'd seen for herself just what material it contained.

"He's gone!" Penelope poked her pretty head in the doorway. "Actually gone—with a serial killer loose in the city! Am I crazy? Or is he?"

Gabrielle's heartbeat drummed so loudly she was sure that Cooper and Penelope had to hear it.

"And there's someone here," Penelope continued as she smoothed back her hair. "Some woman who said she's from the FBI." Her perfectly manicured index finger pointed to Gabrielle. "She keeps asking to see you."

The situation was going from bad to worse.

Cooper was frowning now as he glanced through the doorway.

Penelope smiled at him and she batted her lashes. "The FBI lady is right down the hall, second door on the left."

Cooper hurried out.

Gabrielle crept toward Penelope.

Penelope's smile vanished. "What is going *on?*"

"I'm not sure." She didn't want to mention the EOD to Penelope. Until she figured out more about what was happening, Gabrielle didn't want to risk the other woman's life.

Sure, Penelope was flighty, she was flirty, but she was also one of the few people that Gabrielle counted as a friend.

"What can I do?" Penelope asked. "Hugh's worried, I can tell, and when he worries…*I* worry."

Gabrielle eased out a slow breath. "I need to use your computer, and I need you to keep both Cooper and that FBI agent busy while I do it."

Penelope nodded. "Done." She started to walk away, but then stopped. "When this is all over, you'd better share your byline with me."

"I will," Gabrielle promised. She would have promised just about anything right then.

Penelope bustled away. "Oh, Cooper, the agent is this way, in the conference room…"

They only had one conference room. It was down the hall, in a location a good thirty feet away from Penelope's desk.

Perfect.

Gabrielle all but ran for the empty desk.

An FBI agent. What were the Feds thinking? To get involved in an EOD case like this just wasn't protocol. Mercer should have shut them out immediately.

"Right here," Penelope said, her perfume seeming to swirl in the air around him. She threw open the door. "Agent Noelle Evers, this is Cooper Marshall. He's—" Penelope broke off, tapping her chin thoughtfully. "I think he's working with Gabrielle," she murmured, sounding confused.

"I'm her partner." Cooper crossed the room and offered his hand to the slim redhead. He'd never seen the woman before. Her handshake was brief but solid, and he had the feeling the woman was assessing everything about him—probably because she was.

He glanced over his shoulder, expecting to see Gabrielle.

But Penelope was the only one there, and she was shutting the door.

He pulled away from Agent Evers. "Gabrielle…"

"Oh, she'll be right in. She just stopped by the restroom." Penelope lowered her voice to a conspiratorial whisper. "Talking with Hugh got her emotional. She hated to see the old guy go. He was like a father to her."

Her real father had left her too soon and with a fear of storms and a quest for justice that wouldn't end.

He headed for that door. If she was upset, he wanted to be with her.

Penelope blocked his path. She smiled at him, but her gaze drifted to the FBI agent. "You're here about the D.C. Striker, aren't you?"

The D.C.—

"Yes," Agent Evers said, voice smooth, "I am."

Excitement lit Penelope's gaze. "He's a serial killer, isn't he? Hugh was right about that. You're here because that's what the FBI does. You hunt serials."

"It's one of the many things we do," Agent Evers said, still in that smooth voice that didn't give away any emotion. "We hunt them, and we try to figure out why they do the things that they do."

Her job was very different from his.

He didn't try to understand the killers. He just eliminated them.

GABRIELLE SANK INTO Penelope's chair. Her fingers were trembling as she pushed the flash drive into position.

A few clicks of the mouse, and she had that drive open.

There were two files stored there.

One was titled…*EOD.*

She clicked that one first.

Her gaze darted over the document that opened. It looked like it was a series of notes that Hugh had made.

Ex-military. Covert Ops. Specialize in hostage retrieval and unconventional warfare. Lockwood and McAdams…military records are sealed. Possible EOD agents.

Then Hugh had listed what appeared to be a series of locations and dates. Were those EOD missions?

A phone rang beside her, and Gabrielle jumped. She glanced up, made sure no one was watching her then she went back and clicked on that second file.

That file was labeled *Striker.*

She expected to find more notes within that file. Instead, she found data on—Cooper.

Military records. She had no idea how Hugh had gotten access to these files. Lane had tried and come up empty-handed.

Should have known Hugh would be more resourceful. Somehow, he'd managed to get access to sealed records. Hugh had contacts in all the right—and wrong—places.

She leaned forward as she read the service details. Cooper had joined the Air Force the day after he graduated from Yale. She scanned through the file, noting the commendations, the awards.

There'd been so much training for him. The notations were seemingly endless. Combat Dive School. Army Airborne certification. Military Free Fall Parachutist. He'd been on a special tactics team, and even gone in for Advanced Skills Training.

Her fingers trembled as she clicked the mouse. No wonder the guy could move so soundlessly. He was some kind of super soldier.

Then she saw that Cooper's service ended five years ago. Ended…with an annotation that said Cooper Marshall had been killed in the line of duty.

Her breath choked out.

Killed?

Of course, he hadn't been killed. He was alive and well, and right down the hall in the conference room.

But Hugh had scanned a death certificate. It was right there for her to see, plain as day.

According to those files—files that clearly had a "Confidential" stamp on top of each page, Cooper Marshall was a dead man. There was even a picture of him included. A younger version of Cooper, but definitely him.

She pulled the cursor down and reached the last page of the file.

Hugh had written a note to her.

According to my source, Cooper Marshall is a ghost. Watch your back with him. This story—these murders are all about the EOD.

You're the reporter covering the kills, and all of a sudden, Marshall is shadowing you. He lives in your building, he has access to you…

I think your "guard" knows a whole lot more than we do. Be careful with him.

He was connecting dots that she should have connected herself.

But she'd been blind.

Sometimes, you couldn't see the enemy that was right in front of your face.

Or in your bed.

She scrolled back up and read the details of his "death" one more time. Cooper Marshall had been attempting to rescue a downed pilot behind enemy lines in Afghanistan. He'd gotten that pilot to safety, but Cooper had sustained extensive injuries. He'd died before making it back to base.

Gabrielle's fingers rubbed together as she remembered the scars that marked Cooper's stomach and chest. He had been injured, grievously. But he hadn't died.

"Look, I get that you're into her," Penelope's sharp voice called out, "but give the woman a minute of privacy. I told you already that Gabrielle is going to join us—"

She shut the file and jerked out that flash drive. Her heart raced in her chest as Gabrielle shot up from the chair.

And came face-to-face with a dead man.

Chapter Nine

To be dead, he looked incredibly good. Damn him.

But she had to look shaken because Cooper frowned at her. His hand came up and skimmed her cheek. "What's wrong?"

Have you been lying to me?

She should have put the puzzle pieces together sooner. Gabrielle felt like a fool as she stared up at the man she'd made love with just hours before.

"Gabrielle?"

She slid around him.

Penelope was staring at her with wide eyes, and just behind the entertainment reporter, another woman was also watching her. This woman had dark red hair and a sharp gaze.

Gabrielle's stare swept over the redhead. With that suit, yes, she would've instantly pegged the lady as FBI.

"I have some questions for you," the redhead said.

"What a coincidence," Gabrielle muttered right back. "I've got my share of those, too."

She didn't glance at Cooper as she headed for the conference room. There were too many eyes and ears on them at that moment. It would be far better to have this conversation in private.

Penelope tried to follow them back into the conference room, but the FBI agent firmly shut the door—well, pretty much in the other woman's face.

Gabrielle's eyes narrowed. "I didn't catch your name," she said to the lady.

"Noelle Evers." Noelle offered her a brief smile as she marched toward the conference table. Some folders and a notepad were already spread out there. "And I'm here to learn more about your recent phone call with—"

"The D.C. Striker?" Gabrielle finished for her.

"If that's what you want to call him," Noelle agreed, but she didn't sound impressed with the name.

"She's a profiler," Cooper said as he took the seat near Noelle. "She's here to help the cops catch this guy."

Gabrielle still stood. Her knees had locked on her, so she wasn't even sure that she could sit. "Have the two of you met before?" Suspicion made her ask that question.

And then it happened. Cooper immediately said, "No," but the agent's eyelids jerked, just a little bit. Noelle glanced quickly at Cooper, then away.

Gabrielle's back teeth clenched. A profiler should learn to be better at hiding her emotions.

But that little tell had convinced Gabrielle that she had to press a bit more. "It's all about the EOD."

No emotion crossed Cooper's face. *Oh, so that's when he does that.* The emotion vanished each time he kept a secret from her.

"I don't think I understand," Noelle began carefully. She motioned to the nearby chair. "Why don't you sit down? Then we can really talk."

Gabrielle felt like they were talking just fine. It wasn't like sitting improved a conversation. "Why isn't Detective Carmichael with you? If you're here investigating the killer, shouldn't the local cops be helping you?" But Lane hadn't even given her a heads-up about the profiler.

The whole scene felt wrong. Gabrielle wasn't going to ignore her instincts any longer.

Noelle glanced over at Cooper once more. *What is she doing?* It almost looked as if the profiler were waiting to follow Cooper's lead.

Cooper was staring straight back at Gabrielle. A faint furrow dipped between his brows.

"Right now," Noelle finally said, "the FBI is *assisting* the local authorities. It may become necessary for us to take over the investigation, but at this point, I'm just attempting to gather more data about our suspect."

The answer was smooth, and it sounded rehearsed.

"What did the suspect say, exactly, when he called you, Ms. Harper?" the profiler wanted to know.

"He told me not to trust Cooper. The guy said that Cooper wasn't who I thought."

There was still no expression in his eyes.

"He told me," Gabrielle continued, her chest aching now as she realized that she'd been played by a master, "that if I wasn't careful, I'd trust the wrong man and I'd wind up dead."

Cooper surged to his feet. "Gabrielle—"

"You're EOD." It made sense. So much sense and she felt herself flush. "*That's* why Van's last message was erased at the crime scene. You smeared the blood deliberately, didn't you? To keep your organization quiet. You destroyed evidence."

A muscle jerked in his jaw.

But he didn't deny being EOD. She'd actually expected a denial.

"I think—" Noelle spoke softly as she pulled her files a bit closer "—that we all need to calm down."

"I'm completely calm," Gabrielle said. She was.

An eerie calm that she hadn't expected had settled over her.

Gabrielle pulled out her phone. She held it gripped in her hand. She tilted her head as she studied the profiler. "If I call Detective Carmichael right now, is he going to back up your story? Is he going to even know who you are?"

Noelle hesitated.

That was Gabrielle's answer. "He's not, because you aren't working with the local cops. They aren't the ones who sent you to me." She rolled back her shoulders and forced herself to meet Cooper's stare. "The team that you had searching my apartment—they were from the EOD, weren't they? This guy, this fellow doing the killing, he's one of your agents."

Cooper didn't speak, neither confirming nor denying her charge.

She'd wanted a denial. Crazy, of course, but she'd wanted one.

A woman didn't like to be that wrong about her lover.

She was.

Gabrielle retreated from him and the FBI agent.

Noelle rose. "I really need to ask you more questions. It's imperative that I learn as much about this man as I can."

So that the EOD could catch one of their own?

"He's fixated on you," Noelle continued, as

Gabrielle took another step back. "The fact that he's contacting you gives us an advantage. It means—"

"—that you think you can use me as some kind of bait." Her blinders were definitely off. No wonder Cooper had agreed to be her partner. He was letting her rush out and try to draw the killer's attention.

She'd been live bait in the EOD's trap, and she hadn't even realized it.

"Thanks, but no thanks." Gabrielle spun away and yanked open the door.

"Gabrielle!" Cooper called after her.

Her eyes were tearing up. Knowing that she'd just been a means to an end for him *hurt.*

"Gabrielle? Are you okay?" Penelope asked as she hurried toward her.

"I need to get away," she whispered back.

Penelope handed her a pair of keys. "My car's in the lot."

Then Penelope pushed her away—and rushed toward the conference room door. "Is it my turn for questions? Because I've got tons...."

Penelope was buying her some time by being a distraction. Perfect. Gabrielle gave up trying to look in control—the eerie calm had totally fled. She rushed for the elevator.

Once she slipped inside, she risked a glanced

back and saw Cooper prying himself out of Penelope's grip.

There was emotion on his face right then.

Rage.

The doors slid closed, and Gabrielle sucked in a deep breath.

It looked like the killer had been right about Cooper.

THE BLUE CONVERTIBLE squealed out of the lot just as Cooper reached the parking garage. Damn it, damn it, *damn it!* That interview had gone horribly wrong.

And now Gabrielle was just gone.

How had she found out about him?

He yanked out his phone. Waited with gritted teeth as the phone rang once, twice, then—

"What's wrong?" Dylan Foxx demanded.

What wasn't? A killer was on the loose. The SOB seemed to be going right after Gabrielle, and now, his lover of less than four hours—four hours!—had just run from him as if he were the very devil.

To her, maybe he was. So much for playing the role of the white knight.

"We need containment," he said, though he hated to utter those words. But there wasn't a choice. He couldn't let Gabrielle run from him.

Someone had tipped her off about him. He had to find out just how much she knew.

With the killer targeting her, Gabrielle couldn't just vanish.

He wouldn't let her.

"Gabrielle's on the move," he said, aware that his voice snapped with fury. "Heading west from the *Inquisitor*, driving a blue convertible." He gave Dylan the license plate number.

"Are you sure containment is what you want?" Dylan asked, his tone guarded.

"Those were my orders." If he'd become compromised, if Gabrielle was put in too much danger…

He swallowed and tried to choke back the emotions filling him. "Make sure, *absolutely sure,* that no one hurts her in any way."

He didn't want her to be hurt. He didn't want her to be afraid.

But, judging by the way she'd looked at him just before those elevator doors closed, Gabrielle was *already* both hurt and afraid.

She's scared of me.

Because she'd learned the truth about him.

He was just as much of a killer as the D.C. Striker.

WHERE WAS SHE supposed to go? Back to the brownstone? Retreating to that place really wasn't an option because Cooper lived there, too.

And she couldn't go back to work—he was already waiting back at the *Inquisitor*. Scratch that safe spot from her list.

But she also just couldn't drive aimlessly around the city all night.

Gabrielle braked to a stop at a red light. She glanced in her rearview mirror and saw a pair of headlights approaching.

The red light changed. She turned left.

So did the car behind her.

Gabrielle took a right turn.

The car turned right.

Her fingers tightened their grip on the steering wheel.

She accelerated. That car accelerated, too.

Fear began to thicken within her. Fury had driven her away from Cooper, and she'd foolishly ignored the threats around her. Gabrielle couldn't ignore those threats any longer.

Is it the killer? He'd been watching her before. Had he seen her leave the *Inquisitor*? Without Cooper at her side, the killer might think this was the perfect time for him to strike.

She fumbled and yanked out her phone. For an instant, she thought about calling Cooper.

But, instead, her index finger pushed the button to connect her to Lane. She held her breath. Another red light was up ahead. The light went green. Good. No stopping.

And Lane wasn't answering. Where the heck was he when she needed him?

The green light had turned yellow. In a flash, it went red. She didn't stop. She rushed forward and ran that light.

A horn blared as a truck came right at her. Screaming, she yanked the wheel to the side even as she slammed on the brakes.

The truck missed her by only inches.

Her breath heaved out. She'd dropped her phone. She fumbled, trying to find it.

Someone rapped on her window. "Ma'am?" A woman's voice called. "Ma'am, are you are all right?"

Gabrielle rolled down her window. "Yes, sorry, I—"

The woman wasn't alone. A man stood behind her. His posture was stiff, guarded, and when he shifted his stance a bit, she saw the holster under his arm.

"I'm afraid that you have to come with us, Ms. Harper." The woman's voice wasn't so concerned any longer. It was authoritative and flat.

The truck that had nearly hit Gabrielle moments before had also come to a stop. Two more men were climbing from that vehicle. They headed toward her.

"You're EOD," she said, understanding as a chill seemed to settle over her body.

The woman stared back at her. "There are two ways to do this," the woman said, voice soft.

"Let me guess," Gabrielle muttered as she climbed from the car. "Easy and hard?"

A nod.

The armed man came closer to Gabrielle. The light from the streetlamp glinted off his dark hair. "No one's going to hurt you, ma'am," he assured her. "We're here for your protection." He smiled at her and offered his hand. "My name's Deuce."

Hesitant now, she reached for that hand. "No way is Deuce your real name…"

He yanked her forward. His left hand came up in an instant. Too late, she saw the handcuffs. Before she could jerk away from him, one cuff snapped over her wrist.

"No, it isn't," he agreed softly as he pulled her into his arms. "It's a name for second chances. Maybe you'll give old Cooper one of those chances when this mess is over."

Then she was pretty much dragged into the waiting car. The doors slammed behind her, and the vehicle raced away.

Anger pulsed through her with every mile that passed.

Second chance? *Hell, no.*

COOPER SHOVED OPEN the door to Bruce Mercer's office. *"Where is she?"* The door banged against the wall behind him. Judith Rogers, Mercer's assistant, let out a screech as she tried to jerk him back.

"I told you, Marshall," Judith snapped, sounding as furious as Cooper felt, "the boss is working! You can't just barge in there!"

Yeah, he could. He had.

Mercer glanced up from his computer. "If you're referring to Gabrielle Harper, she's here, of course. Where else would she be? Especially since *you're* the one who told us to pick her up."

Cooper's hands fisted. "I want to see her." He ignored Judith's attempts to pull him back. For a small woman, she was surprisingly strong. Just not strong enough.

Mercer glanced at his assistant. "It's okay, Judith. I needed to talk with Cooper anyway."

"Yes, well," Judith stopped trying to drag Cooper out and she gave an annoyed sniff, "he needs to learn how to *not* barge into an office."

She stomped away and slammed the door quite loudly on her way out.

Cooper didn't move. "Gabrielle." Ordering that containment on her had been the hardest thing he'd ever done. He knew she had to be furious, had to feel betrayed. He needed to get to her and try to explain what was happening.

"We have her on the fourth floor."

His eyes widened. They had prisoner rooms on that floor. "Tell me that she's not—"

"Easy." Mercer lifted his hands. "She's just in an interrogation room. Deuce is guarding the door."

Guarding the door? Right. More like he was guarding *her* in order to make sure that Gabrielle didn't try to escape.

"We don't have a lot of options here," Mercer said with a shake of his head. "I can't have a reporter exposing the EOD."

Cooper tried to keep his control in place. Hard, when he already knew it had fractured. Actually, his control had been weakening since the first moment he'd met Gabrielle. "Let me talk to her."

Mercer's brows rose. "Are you so sure she will want to talk with you? I think your charm might have run its course with the reporter."

The fractures grew deeper. "I shouldn't have made that a request," Cooper threw back. "I should have said…I'm *talking to her.*"

Mercer stood then. He wasn't quite as tall as Cooper, and even though Mercer had to be pushing his late fifties, he was still in top shape. "I think you're forgetting a few things, Agent Marshall," Mercer told him.

"I'm not forgetting anything." He wasn't going to let the EOD hurt Gabrielle.

"Yes, you are." Mercer marched around the

desk and came toward him. "It was the EOD who saved your hide in Afghanistan. My team who pulled *you* out. Otherwise, you really would have been dead. We went there to find you when you were being held captive. We got you out."

"So now I owe you." But what about Gabrielle? He owed her, so much.

She's changed me.

Mercer's eyes were narrowed as he studied Cooper. "You're not the same agent anymore."

He didn't want to argue with Mercer. He just wanted to get down to the fourth floor.

Mercer sighed. "You can all fall so fast, and you don't even see the danger until it's too late."

"She's not a danger. I can convince her to keep the news about the EOD quiet. Let me talk to her, explain things—" She'd been running away before. He hadn't known where she was going. He'd been worried that she might have other contacts in the press that she would talk with about her new discoveries.

He'd also been worried that the rogue would get her. Fear had burned like acid within him. Cooper hadn't been able to stand the thought that Gabrielle was in the killer's path, unprotected, vulnerable.

"I think you're compromised on this one," Mercer told him bluntly. "You aren't the best agent for the job."

"What?" There was no way he'd let Mercer bench him. "*I'm* the one who's been monitoring her. I'm the one who kept the EOD out of the news. I'm the one—"

"—who slept with the reporter."

Every muscle in Cooper's body locked down. "How the hell do you know that?"

"You think that you were the only agent I had keeping tabs on her? Deuce has been watching her place. My agents always have backup close by."

"Then I guess he got a real eyeful." His control wasn't fracturing. It was splintering.

While Mercer was his same old cold self. "Emotions cloud judgment. I know what I'm talking about here."

"You mean your daughter?" They were alone, so Cooper decided to cut right to the chase. He'd worked closely with Mercer before, and he knew the man's secrets. "You let your love for Cassidy compromise you—and you nearly got her killed."

"I *did* get my wife killed," Mercer shocked him by saying. Grief flickered in his eyes. "And when I realized how dangerous I was to those closest to me, I backed the hell off." Mercer's gaze turned shuttered once more as it drifted over Cooper's face. "I backed away from the only family that I had left because I wanted to protect them."

And what? He was supposed to follow in Mercer's footsteps? Hell, no. Cooper would make his own way in this world, and he'd make his own choices. "If you think I'm backing away from Gabrielle, you're dead wrong—"

"I backed away," Mercer's voice cut though his words, "because I thought I was protecting them. But it turns out, my leaving just meant that I wasn't there when they needed me the most."

Cooper blinked. Okay. Now *that* he hadn't been expecting. "I thought you were going to say I should stay away from her. You said emotions compromise agents."

"They do. So be aware of that danger, but, no, I'm not telling you to back away from her." Mercer turned away and paced toward the window. "I had a sister. She was younger than me—ten years younger. So beautiful and sweet. After I lost my wife, I didn't want to run the risk of losing her, too."

Mercer had *never* gotten this personal with him. As far as Cooper knew, Mercer didn't get personal with anyone.

"I didn't want one of my enemies to get close to my sister," Mercer said, gazing out of that window. "I had—still have—so many folks who'd love to hurt me, and they'd do it in an instant by taking out the ones I care about in this world."

Like a sister.

Mercer's shoulders were stiff and straight, his spine tense. "But it wasn't an enemy who took her." Sadness deepened his tone. "Cancer did that. It came in an instant. It took her from me too soon. I blinked, and she was just—gone."

Cooper rubbed his chest, pushing at the ache that was always there when he remembered his mother. "I'm sorry. My…my mother died of cancer." He could understand the pain Mercer felt.

"Did she?" The sadness deepened in Mercer's voice. "I'm sorry for your loss, too, son. So sorry…" Mercer's voice trailed away. He didn't look back at Cooper, but stared straight ahead. Cooper could see Mercer's reflection in the window's glass. "We do our best in this world. We try to protect those we love. We try to make a difference, but, in the end, we can still fail. We can still hurt. And we can still lose…."

I don't want to lose Gabrielle.

"There's one lesson I've learned. If you want to be happy in this world, then you need to find the one thing that you care about the most. When you find it, you move heaven and hell and you do *anything* you can to protect that thing." Mercer finally turned toward him. "Do you understand what I'm saying to you?"

He did. Mercer wasn't pulling him from the case. He was clearing him to do anything necessary—*to protect Gabrielle.* He hadn't expected that response from Mercer. Cooper had thought that he'd have to fight in order to stay at her side.

"Go on, get down to that fourth floor. And remember, if you need anything...day or night, you call me. You can count on me to be there for you, Marshall."

Everyone was wrong about Mercer. He wasn't the cold, emotionless director.

Cooper spun for the door.

"Annalise should've had a different ending." Mercer's words were a low mumble.

Yet Cooper heard him clearly, and he froze. "How do you know my mother's name?"

Silence. Then, "Do you really think you'd get an offer to join the EOD without me reviewing every single detail of your life?"

So Mercer had already known about his mother's cancer *before* he'd told his own story. Maybe that was why the director had revealed his past to Cooper. *He knew I'd understand.*

"The fourth floor's waiting," Mercer reminded him.

Cooper didn't want Gabrielle waiting any longer.

THE DOOR CLICKED shut behind Cooper.

Mercer glanced down. His hands were shaking. When he'd been talking with Cooper, the old pain had come back. The hurt, for what he'd lost.

Annalise. He hadn't needed to dig into Cooper's past to learn about her.

He could just close his eyes and picture sweet Anna. That long blond hair. Her wide smile and glinting eyes—the same shade as Cooper's.

She should've had a perfect life. A long life.

"I'm doing my best to protect him," Mercer whispered. By staying away, he'd missed out on being close when Annalise needed him.

So he'd made sure to keep a good eye on Cooper. When the man had been taken in Afghanistan, Mercer immediately ordered his agents to sweep in for a rescue mission.

Cooper had a love of danger—a love that put him in too much jeopardy.

If Cooper could love something more than that wild rush of adrenaline, if he could love *someone* else more…

Then the man might actually have a chance of living the life Annalise would have wanted for him.

Cooper just had to feel a deep connection for someone else. He had to *need* someone more than he needed the next mission.

Judging by the rage and fear that Mercer had seen in his eyes, the reporter was making Cooper feel that connection, all right.

Now, the trick was going to be actually keeping her alive—and convincing Gabrielle Harper that Cooper deserved a second chance with her.

Luckily, Mercer had plenty of resources at his disposal.

Besides, if Cooper was anything like his mother had been, the boy should be able to work his charm.

Mercer would just see how that charm worked on Gabrielle.

THE DOOR SQUEAKED OPEN.

Gabrielle's head lifted. Her eyes locked on the man who'd just entered her little prison.

Betrayal stabbed in her gut. She jumped to her feet, but the cuff around her left wrist—the cuff that was currently attaching her to the table leg—prevented her from charging across the room at Cooper.

He stilled. "I didn't realize… I'll get that cuff off you."

He'd better do a whole lot more than just that.

Cooper turned back around toward the door. The dark-haired, green-eyed agent—the one who'd called himself Deuce—stood behind Cooper.

"Give me the keys," Cooper demanded.

Deuce whistled as he rocked back on his heels. "Are you sure that you want to do that, man? She's likely to go right for your throat."

"The keys," Cooper gritted, and he opened his hand.

Deuce tossed him the keys. “It’s a good thing you had combat training.” His stare swept toward Gabrielle. “I’ll just…ah…leave you two alone.” He backed out of the room.

Cooper hurried toward her.

She was so furious Gabrielle didn’t even know where to start. She had to bite her lip to hold back the furious yells that wanted to erupt.

His fingers closed around her wrist. His touch was warm and solid and— “You really do look good for a dead man,” she told him, her eyes angry slits.

The cuff clicked open. He didn’t let her wrist go. Instead, he lightly rubbed the flesh. She knew he had to feel the frantic race of her pulse beneath his fingers.

“How did you find out?” While her voice had been heated, his was soft.

“Sources, Cooper. Sources. I have them, you know.” She wasn’t about to throw Hugh under the bus. It was a good thing she’d taken the liberty of hiding the flash drive in Penelope’s car. Otherwise, she would’ve lost that evidence during her little confinement time. That flash drive was her ace in the hole. It was her—

“They found the flash drive,” Cooper told her. “And, soon enough, I *will* have the name of your source.”

Could the night get any worse? “I guess you

like going through my things." She snatched her hand back from him. "I figured it out, you know, that mysterious crash of my computer days ago… that was you, right? You and your EOD buddies."

She wanted him to deny it. To tell her that she was wrong. He hadn't really snuck into her house and sabotaged her system.

But he nodded.

Gabrielle took a step away from him as she sucked in a deep gulp of air.

"Let me explain," Cooper began. To the right, a large mirror stretched along the wall and threw their reflections back at them. She looked tired and scared and angry.

And he, damn him, looked strong and determined and too handsome.

The fact that he looked so controlled just increased her fury. "Explain? I'm a prisoner! This shouldn't be happening to me. I've got rights, but those rights were ignored when your buddies dragged me in here." She tossed her hands into the air as she backed away from him. "I wasn't Mirandized—"

"—because you aren't charged with anything," he muttered, yanking a hand through his blond hair.

"This is kidnapping." She wondered if she could run past him and make a break out of the door. They'd blindfolded her before she was brought into this building. She had no idea where she was—or even *if* she was still in D.C. They'd seemed to drive around for hours in that car.

And she'd been terrified every moment.

Cooper exhaled. "Believe it or not, you're here for your protection."

A bitter laugh escaped her. "I'll go with the 'not' option on there. I'm here because I found out your secret and you don't want me telling the world what I know."

He stalked toward her.

Coward that she was, Gabrielle backed up even more. She backed up until there was no place left to go, and she hit the wall.

Cooper kept coming.

His hands rose and flattened on either side of her head, caging her between him and the hard wall. He wasn't touching her, a very good thing, because his touch just twisted things within her even more.

"This isn't about me," he said, staring deeply into her eyes. "It's about the agents in the field. About the work that they do that requires secrecy. You can't print what you've learned about the EOD. You do that, and you compromise their lives."

"And what if the EOD is killing? What then?" She threw her accusation at him. She wanted to hurt him as she was hurting. *I trusted you.* More, she'd started to fall for the guy when he'd just been playing her.

She and Lane hadn't worked out because he wanted to put her in a glass bubble and stop her from doing everything that she loved. They'd crashed and burned fast because she hadn't wanted to give up the person who she was in order to please him. The breakup had hurt, but—

With Cooper, the pain was worse. So much worse. She'd really thought that he'd been on her side. A true partner, an equal. She'd believed that he supported what she was doing.

When he'd been sabotaging her all along.

She swallowed and tried to calm her racing heart. "Van McAdams left a very clear message—"

"Van *was* EOD," Cooper revealed, voice rumbling. "So was Lockwood. Why do you think I'm on the case? They weren't active-duty EOD any longer, but they were still *ours*. I'm trying to find their killer, and I'm working to make sure that no more agents go down."

There was more there. She'd already figured the pieces out. When she'd been cuffed in this room, Gabrielle had been given plenty of time to think. "One of your own is killing. He scaled McAdams's building, right? He did it, the same way that you told Carmichael *you* could do it. He got easy access to those men because they knew him. They trusted him. *He's one of yours.*"

And that terrified her. Because it sure sounded like EOD agents were trained killing machines.

"The killer is a rogue," Cooper said as he leaned in even closer. "He killed two other agents that you don't even know about. He took them out, then he started going after civilians."

Her breath caught. "Kylie Archer."

"From what we can tell, she was the first non–EOD agent." His face hardened. "The agents you don't know about yet were Jessica Flintwood and Frank Malone. They were partners, a team."

Just like she'd been partners with Cooper.

"He killed Jessica first. He slit her throat, just like with the others. Then he took out Frank a few weeks later."

Her eyelids flickered. "He kills a woman, then a man." But…with Kylie and Lockwood, they'd been a couple. So had Melanie and Van. Her gaze widened. "Were Jessica and—ah, Frank, were they involved?"

He frowned at her. "What?"

"Were they involved?" She could see the pattern, it was right there. "A couple. Just like the others."

"I don't know…" His head cocked to the right. "They worked together closely. Agents aren't supposed to cross that line, so if they were, they would've kept it quiet."

"But he found out." It made sense to her, but Cooper was still frowning. "He's targeting the women first, then going after their men." She didn't know why, but the killer had a pattern, a routine that he was following."

"Right now," his voice roughened, "I'm worried he's going after *you.*" A grim pause, then Cooper said, "He's calling *you*, breaking into *your* house, targeting *you.*"

His words made her afraid, but she wasn't about to give into fear then.

"But it's not going to happen," he promised her. "Because I am not going to let anyone hurt you."

Before she could say anything else, his head lowered, and his mouth pressed to hers.

NOELLE EVERS JOLTED. "That's it. That's why he does it!"

Deuce Porter glanced at her. "Ma'am, that's a kiss." His smile was wide. "Maybe we should step out of observation and give those two some privacy."

Mercer had sent her down to watch the interaction between Cooper and Gabrielle, because he'd thought Gabrielle might speak more freely to that agent.

Mercer had been right.

But what she'd learned, the profile that was developing before her, it wasn't what she'd expected. "I have to see Mercer."

Deuce's brows climbed. "I thought you'd be talking to all of us. You know…figuring out which one of us has snapped and gone crazy." He shrugged. "Though you'll no doubt have a hard time picking just one candidate. I think we're all a little crazy."

"I know what he's doing," she said, excitement growing within her. "*Why* he's doing it." The why was the most important part. Once you understood a killer's motivation, that made the perp vulnerable. You could manipulate him then.

Trap him.

She hurried for the door.

"Why?" Deuce asked, the question a growl. "I'd like to know why he killed my friend. Lockwood and I—we worked plenty of missions together. He was a good man. He didn't deserve to go down like that."

She couldn't tell the agent why. She was only supposed to talk with Mercer. Just him.

Noelle opened the door and hurried into the hallway. She was in such a hurry to get to Mercer that she slammed straight into the man standing there.

Big, strong, with midnight-black hair and dark,

golden eyes, the fellow caught her in an instant and held her in a steady grip.

"Dragon, you don't want to be getting too close to her..." Deuce warned from behind her. "She's Mercer's profiler. She's here to find out which one of us has gone psychotic."

Dragon?

The man before her slowly released his hold on her.

"Of course, after what happened to you on that last mission, maybe *you* should be talking to her," Deuce mused. "How many of your captors did you kill? And all without even a single weapon."

She shouldn't be hearing this. She should be rushing for the elevator and hurrying up to see Mercer.

Instead, Noelle found it hard to look away from that man's golden eyes. She frowned at him, a pulse of recognition stirring within her. "Have we met before, agent?"

His lips curved in the faintest of smiles. "I've seen you, but I don't think you've seen me, Doctor."

Then he turned around and headed down the hallway. His movements were absolutely soundless, and he moved with an easy, catlike grace.

Deuce came to her side. "Be careful with him," he murmured. "I mean it, Agent Evers. I've never seen a more deadly agent, and I've been here for almost seven years now. That guy doesn't get close to anyone, and when he kills..." His breath rushed out. "We're supposed to have remorse, aren't we? We're supposed to be more than just machines, following orders." His hands shoved into his pockets. "People should matter more than just mission orders."

Yes, they should.

She cleared her throat and hurried for the elevator. Noelle slipped inside.

She wasn't in that elevator alone.

The man Deuce had called "Dragon" was there. He didn't speak as they rode up that elevator together.

Goose bumps rose on her arms.

There was something about him.

One look, and he'd scared her.

One look, and he'd—

The elevator chimed. The doors opened. Noelle nearly tripped as she rushed out and toward the desk of Mercer's assistant.

Before she could even ask to see the director, he was there, frowning at her. "What's wrong? What happened?"

It wasn't what *had* already happened that made her fear so much.

They went back into Mercer's office. He closed the door, sealing them inside. She tried to calm her racing heartbeat. "Kylie Archer was involved with Keith Lockwood."

His brow furrowed. "I already told you—"

"Your rogue killed her in order to get at Lockwood. She was the easy kill, the one who wouldn't expect his attack. Then, while Lockwood was grieving, while he was weak with his loss, the killer went after him."

The pairs made so much sense to her now. Once she'd realized that the first two victims were also intimately connected, she understood why the rogue was taking out the women first. *Because he wants the men to suffer more. He wants them to mourn for what they've lost.*

Mercer's expression tightened. "He did the same thing with Melanie and Van."

Yes, he had. "He's killing the women, almost executing them, and I think he is doing it just to make their lovers suffer. He wants them to hurt, to grieve. When they're broken, then he goes in—"

"—for the kill," Mercer finished.

"He's doing it again. It's already in motion. I can see it now." Her words were coming out too fast, so she tried to slow them down. "Gabrielle Harper. He's not talking to her because she's the reporter investigating his kills. He's focused on her because of her relationship to Cooper." A very personal relationship, judging by what she'd just seen in that interrogation room. "He's already told us—we just didn't realize—Gabrielle is his next target. And, once she's dead…"

His voice and face grim, Mercer said, "He'll go after Cooper."

Chapter Ten

He shouldn't be kissing her. He should be taking things slower, trying to soothe her. Trying to mend the fences that he'd destroyed.

But he needed her. So much.

His body pressed against hers, and Cooper knew that Gabrielle had to feel the force of his arousal. For her.

Everything was for her.

Her hands flew up and grabbed his shoulders. He tensed, expecting her to push him away.

Then her mouth parted beneath his. Her tongue met his. She kissed him back with the same raw, wild need that he felt.

In that moment, she nearly brought him to his knees.

Everything was going to be all right. Gabrielle understood why he'd kept his true identity secret. They could go back to the way things had been before.

Her taste made him light-headed, desperate for more.

His hands locked around her. He pulled her against him, holding the curve of her hips.

But then she shoved against him. "No." Her voice was husky but brimming with anger. "Just because I want you, you *aren't* going to get away with what you've done to me."

Tears glittered in her gorgeous eyes. Actual tears.

"I trusted you. You broke into my home. You destroyed evidence."

"I was following orders." Those words seemed hollow to his ears.

She edged away from him. "That's what you're still doing. Let me guess…whoever runs this place told you to come in here and charm me again?"

He wasn't touching that one.

She laughed, and the sound wasn't like her at all. Gabrielle wasn't that bitter. Gabrielle was open, happy.

"This isn't going to work. *We* aren't going to work." She headed for the door.

He had to stop her. Cooper hated to do it, but he stepped into her path.

Her head tilted back as she stared up at him. "What are you going to do?" Gabrielle asked him as she swiped a hand over her cheek. "Handcuff me again?"

"No." *Stay calm. Stay calm.* But it was hard because he felt like his world was unraveling before his eyes. "I'm going to make sure that you're free to go, but in return, you have to do something for me."

"I get to just walk out of here?" Doubt was plain on her face.

"We have your flash drive. You don't know anything else about the EOD, nothing concrete. And if you try to cover the story, you *will* put lives at risk." He crossed his arms over his chest and studied her. "That's not who you are. You bring justice to families. You don't go out and try to hurt anyone."

"You actually sound as if you know me."

"I do." Better than he'd known any other lover.

"I wish I could say the same about you."

Hit. The woman was lethal with her words.

"But I don't know you," Gabrielle continued on fiercely. "I feel like I'm staring straight at a stranger."

"You're staring at your lover." She wasn't going to deny that—deny *them.*

She gave a hard shake of her head. "I'm staring at an EOD agent who's done nothing but lie to me."

"I'm the one who got you out of Lockwood's place so the cops wouldn't find you there. I'm the one who's been helping you." She might not want to see the truth now, but sooner or later, she'd have to look past her rage.

I want sooner.

"We can keep helping each other," he told her, trying to keep the desperate edge out of his words. "We make a good team, Gabrielle, and that doesn't have to end. Agree to drop any inquiries into the EOD, and I'll talk to my boss. I'll get you out of here."

Her eyelashes flickered. "Why did I get dragged into this place? If I already had an EOD agent with me day *and* night, then why did I—" She broke off as her eyes widened. *"You."*

Hell. This was about to go from bad to worse.

"*You* were chasing after me. I ran from you, and you called in your backup, didn't you?"

His back teeth had locked. "A killer is out there. After *you.* What was I supposed to do? Let you run straight into danger?"

"You don't even know that he's after me—"

The door opened behind Cooper.

"Yes," Bruce Mercer's distinct voice said clearly. "We do know that the killer is after you, Ms. Harper. And if you want to keep living, then I would suggest that you calm down and get used to the idea of working with the EOD."

THE PROFILER WAS too damn good.

She'd been poking her head in where it didn't belong, getting too close.

Trying to learn too much about me.

He hadn't thought Mercer would pull in an outsider to hunt him.

He'd underestimated the bastard.

He hurried down the hallway. Other agents were working, barely glancing his way.

They knew that a killer was among them. Did they care?

No, because we're all killers.

Some just hid that truth a bit better than others.

He rounded the corner. His gaze cut to the office on the right.

She was there.

He sucked in a deep breath and walked closer to her door.

Then he heard her laugh.

Rachel Mancini wasn't alone, and there was only one man that ever made her laugh.

A few more steps and he saw that Dylan Foxx was leaning over her, putting his body too close to hers.

The fool gave away too much when he looked at Rachel. He made the same mistakes that Frank Malone had made with his Jessica.

His glances were too possessive, his posture too protective.

Rachel might not feel the same way that Dylan did, but what did that matter?

He needed a distraction, someone else for the profiler and Mercer to focus on.

He'd change the order of his game. Move his pieces around the board a bit.

Rachel glanced up then. The smile was still on her pretty face as she looked at him.

Time for my attack.

He stepped into her office.

COOPER BRACED HIS body in front of Gabrielle's. "You shouldn't be here," he said flatly.

Wait, who was he talking to? Gabrielle peered around his shoulder. The older man with the gray at his temples or Agent Evers?

Gabrielle pushed onto her tiptoes and tried to see a bit better.

"No." Cooper spun around and grabbed her shoulders. "The less you know about him, the better off you are."

Her heart slammed into her ribs. Just when she'd thought that things surely couldn't get any worse…

"Don't be so certain," the man replied. "I'm here to offer Ms. Harper a very special deal, one that I think she'll accept, if she wants to keep living."

She met that man's stare, feeling a wave of shock sweep over her. "Are you threatening me?"

The man was handsome, tall, fit…and dangerous. The danger clung to him like a second skin.

Noelle Evers stood beside him, and she kept glancing nervously at the fellow.

"I don't threaten," the man said simply. "Threats are a waste of time. It's actions that matter."

Cooper dropped his hold on her.

Gabrielle shook her head. "Who are you?"

"Let's just say I'm an old friend of your boss's."

Doubtful. "Are you the same 'friend' who convinced Hugh to take his little out-of-town trip?"

He flashed a grim smile. "Guilty."

Okay. Her breath was icy in her lungs. She wasn't just looking at another agent. "You're the one in charge here, huh?"

His head inclined.

"You're in danger," Noelle said, her words sharp. "I think you're the killer's next victim."

Was that true? Or just the EOD's way of trying to keep Gabrielle in line?

"I believe that he's going to come after you—" Noelle advanced toward her "—in order to hurt Cooper."

Her temples were throbbing. "How would targeting me do anything to Cooper?"

Beside her, Cooper growled. Actually growled.

Her gaze shot to him.

"It would do plenty." He'd never looked at her quite that way before. The intensity in his eyes scorched through her.

For a moment, Gabrielle was at a loss.

"You need protection." The big boss seemed definite on this point. "The local cops can't handle this killer—"

"—because he's someone you trained, and now you can't control him?" Yep. There she went. Saying perhaps a wee bit too much to a man who could probably make her vanish in five seconds flat. Actually, he'd *already* made her vanish.

Mr. Mysterious stared at her.

Just stared.

She stared back, not about to let him think he was pushing her around—even if he was.

"I want this rogue stopped," he said clearly. "And I also want you to keep living. Despite what you may believe about me, my organization doesn't target innocents. We *save* them."

"The killer isn't saving anyone, and he's part of *your* organization."

Mr. Mysterious glowered at her.

Noelle focused on Gabrielle. "He's called you. He's broken into your house."

Gabrielle's eyes darted to Cooper, then back to Noelle. "There seems to be a lot of that going around."

Noelle's lips tightened. "The next move he makes could be to kill you."

She wasn't in the mood to die.

Cooper's boss straightened his, well, *already* ramrod-straight shoulders. "There are over two dozen of my agents currently working undercover missions. They are putting their lives on the line in order to protect innocents." That gaze of his was practically arctic. "Before we go any farther, I have to know that I can trust you, Ms. Harper."

Wait. He doubted *her?* "I'm not the one who's been pretending here!"

"Gabrielle," Cooper snapped out.

"Don't 'Gabrielle' me." She marched right up to Mr. Mysterious. "Look, I'm not interested in blowing the covers of your agents. I'm interested in stopping this killer. I made a promise to Kylie Archer's little brother. I told him I'd do everything possible to give his sister justice, and I mean to do exactly that."

"Even if the price you pay for that justice is your own life?" The man asked her. "Don't you think that price is too steep?" His gaze slid to Cooper. "I can already tell you, *he* thinks it's too high."

"I don't plan on dying," she managed to say. "I'm not blowing the covers of your agents, and I'm not winding up in a morgue." She paused. "Happy now? Can I go?"

"Once you agree to let Agent Marshall stick to your side—24/7—yes, then I'll be...happy."

She wasn't sure anything could truly make this guy happy. "Why are we even playing this game?

You're going to stick me with your agent, no matter what I say."

His eyes seemed to warm as he studied her. "Cooper was right, you know. The two of you did make a good team."

Her gaze snapped to the mirror. She'd been in enough police stations to know how those two-way viewing mirrors worked. "I wondered how much of an audience we had."

Apparently, a pretty big one.

Gabrielle sighed. To get out of that place, she'd be ready to promise plenty. "I agree to the deal."

"You won't regret it," Cooper promised softly.

She already did. Actually, there were quite a few things she regretted concerning Cooper Marshall, but she'd shared enough with these folks.

"We're going to be monitoring your phone line. If he calls you again, we'll trace his call," the big boss said.

"I'm surprised you weren't already monitoring me," she muttered.

Cooper's cheeks flushed. "We were," he confessed. "After the first phone call—"

"Right, I got it." She shoved back her hair. "So I'm a target, the killer is coming, and I'm supposed to be the bait to lure him out. I think I'm up to speed now." Though she'd rather not be just then.

"You're not bait," Cooper immediately denied. His arm brushed against hers. "You're my partner. I keep telling you that. We're working together from here on out."

She wanted to believe him.

She couldn't.

"Cooper Marshall is the only EOD agent that you should trust," the boss told her.

Her eyebrows lifted at that warning.

"The others you've met—Rachel, Dylan—I don't want you alone with any of them. Cooper was out of the country when I first became aware of the rogue. Cooper is clear." Spoken flatly. "Trust him."

Noelle nodded. "And I'm going to finish working up my profile. Understanding why the rogue is killing is key. He's targeting the women first for a special reason. I—I think it's even possible that the man we're after lost someone that he cared about, and now he's determined to take out his rage on the other agents. He wants them to feel the same pain, the same agony that he experienced."

Cooper frowned. "He's punishing *us?*"

"By taking away what you value most," the boss told him. "So remember the advice I gave you. Do whatever is necessary, Cooper, to protect what matters most."

GABRIELLE COULD ONLY see darkness. Another blindfold covered her eyes. Only this time, Cooper had been the one to blindfold her.

She might have gotten an audience with the mysterious EOD boss, but apparently she didn't have enough clearance to learn the EOD's address.

A door shut. Cooper took her hand, as he'd already done several times. A car engine growled, and then she heard the distinct sound of wheels rolling away.

Their ride—heading back to the EOD.

She waited, expecting Cooper to remove the blindfold.

When he didn't, she tensed. *What's next?*

His fingers curled around her elbow, and he led her forward. He guided her up a set of steps.

A wind chime sounded. A familiar sound. It was *her* wind chime.

Her hands lifted, and Gabrielle ripped that blindfold away.

They were back at the brownstone.

So much for not being bait.

Cooper stood beside her. He stared at her with wary eyes. The guy was right to be wary. The darkness of the night surrounded him, and the only light spilled from the porch. In that harsh light, his face seemed carved from granite. The shadows and darkness surrounded him.

He opened the front door.

Right. They couldn't just stand out there. They'd no doubt make a perfect target if they did that.

She hurried inside and immediately went toward the stairs.

"Gabrielle." He caught her hand, stilling her before she could escape. "My place. Day and night, remember?"

Like she could forget.

Seething, she followed him. She understood why the EOD needed to be kept secret. She understood that he was doing his job.

But why did he make love to me?

That part, she didn't get it. The idea that he'd just been using her, trying to get close to her so that he could gather intel…that part hurt the most.

She made her way into his apartment, too aware of every move that he made. He shut the door behind her. She took five more steps—then froze. "Are we being watched?" The way she'd been watched back at the EOD?

"We could be under surveillance," he admitted as he came toward her.

Not what she wanted to hear. "Video equipment? Audio surveillance?" The whole place could be bugged. "Did they see what we did?" Her voice was a horrified whisper.

If he'd let the other agents watch them…she felt her cheeks burn.

Cooper gave a hard shake of his head. "Do you think I would let that happen? That was about me and you, and no one else."

Her breath rushed out in relief. She turned away.

"Don't treat me like a stranger."

Her hands trembled. She rubbed her fingers over her jean-clad thighs. "Isn't that what you are? I mean, I lay down next to my lover—a living, breathing man I trusted, but then I found out that he was some secret agent, and that he'd supposedly died on a mission in Afghanistan."

"I *should* have died. I was shot to hell and back—"

The image of his scars flashed through her mind.

"But somehow Mercer found out about me."

Mercer. She filed that name into her vault.

"I don't even know how I showed up on the guy's radar," Cooper continued. "He found out about me. He came for me. His Shadow Agents burst onto the scene, they dragged me out of that hell, and they brought me back to life." His shoulders rolled back as if he were trying to push away the memory. "But by that point, everyone on my original team already thought I was dead. And it wasn't like I had any family. I never knew my dad.

Cancer took my mother when I was a teenager. Hell, I already felt like a ghost, so when Mercer made me an offer, I took it."

He turned on the lamp near him, and more light spilled across the room.

"I've worked with the EOD since then. The agents do their missions, and like Mercer said, we save lives."

It wasn't that simple. "One of the agents is taking lives."

He paced toward her. "And it's *our* job to stop him. I didn't expect you to get involved. You were my neighbor. The sexy girl who slipped into my fantasies. I'd known only blood and death until you." He swallowed. "Then you were in my world, looking so beautiful and smelling of lilacs."

She had lilac body lotion. A gift from Penelope.

"But then I found you at Lockwood's apartment. You were in the wrong place. Hell, you almost walked *right* in on me."

Another piece of the puzzle snapped into place. *He'd been in Lockwood's apartment.* "That was why the door was open." He'd been there, first, before her. "You broke in to that apartment."

He nodded, and kept coming closer to her. "No one had heard from Lockwood in days. I knew something was wrong, and I had to get inside to him."

"How did you get out—" Gabrielle began, then

stopped because she realized what he'd done. "You scaled the building."

Another nod. "The same way that the killer did."

Because they were the same—the same training, the same deadly instincts.

"Everything changed when you got involved," he said again. "Protecting you became a priority for me. I only called the EOD in because I didn't have a choice. I knew the killer had you in his sights—after that phone call, how could there be any doubt? It was too risky for you to go off alone."

"You thought I was going to blow your cover. You thought—"

"I thought that if anything happened to you, I'd go crazy." He was right in front of her. Not touching her, but seeming to surround her.

She shook her head. "You don't have to paint some fake story about how you feel, okay? You had orders. You had—"

"I'd had *you,*" he told her bluntly. The burn in her cheeks got even worse. "I'd had you, and there was no going back. It wasn't about one night—I want more than that from you. I want a hell of a lot more."

The first time she'd met him, Gabrielle had known that he was out of her league. Too intense. Too fierce.

And, damn him, too sexy.

"I'll have you again," Cooper said.

Her jaw dropped.

"Because you want me. You're angry, rightly so, but you still want me." He took her hand. Put it over his chest. Over the heart that she could feel racing so frantically. "And I want you. More than I've ever wanted another woman. The way I feel for you isn't about a mission. It's not about anything, but us."

Was he about to kiss her? She didn't want him to kiss her. Oh, dang it, she was the liar now. She wanted his mouth more than breath right then, but she was also scared.

Of him.

Of the way he made her feel.

Of making a mistake. *I'm already in too deep with him.*

"What do I need to do—" his words were a deep, sexy rumble "—to get you back again?"

"I don't want secrets." Her words surprised her. She'd meant to pull away from him.

Hadn't she?

So why was she edging closer? And why did she continue, saying, "I don't want any lies. I might not have your EOD clearance, but that doesn't mean you get to jerk me around." His heart was still racing beneath her touch. Only fair, considering her heart felt as if it would jump out of her chest. "And if we're partners, really partners, then that means you don't leave me behind. We work together. We share everything."

He was staring straight down at her.

She just didn't want…*secrets.*

"I should be running from you right now," Gabrielle said. That would have been the smart thing to do, but her heart wasn't interested in smart. Her heart just wanted her to be close to him.

He'd gotten past her defenses. He'd gotten to her. She was afraid that she wouldn't be the same ever again.

"If you ran, I'd follow." His voice was deeper, sending a shiver over her spine. "I think I might just follow you any place you go."

Gabrielle couldn't pull her gaze from his. His stare burned. "Tell me…tell me that you didn't sleep with me for the case."

His hands lifted and curled around her hips. They seemed to singe her through her clothes. "I slept with you because you were driving me out of my mind. Fantasies weren't enough to keep me sane. What happened between us had nothing to do with the case."

That was good. That was— "If you ever have me handcuffed again, you are going to have some serious trouble on your hands."

He smiled at her. A smile that reached his eyes and made her heart ache. "Sweetheart, if I handcuff you again, you'll be in my bed—and trouble will be the last thing I get."

That was…*oh.* His mouth took hers. She let go of her fear and her anger because right then, they didn't matter.

She wasn't sure how much time they had left together. With the killer out there, there was no way to determine their future.

So she forgot about the future.

She let go of the past.

Gabrielle just held on to him.

His tongue thrust into her mouth. His hands curled around her hips and lifted her up against the hard bulge of his arousal. She met him, kissing him back with a fierce desire that grew and grew within her.

She'd never been the kind of girl to get swept off her feet…

Cooper raised her higher in his arms.

...until now.

He took a few steps, and her back hit the wall. He didn't release her. He kept her pinned there, and she twisted, arching against his hips.

Need rose to a feverish pitch within her as his mouth trailed down her neck. He licked her, kissed the curve of her throat. Had her gasping and digging her nails into his shoulders.

"I can't get enough of you." One of his hands yanked her shirt over her head. He held her easily.

Sometimes, she forgot just how strong he was. He lifted her a few more inches, and his mouth pressed to the curve of her breast, right above the lace of her bra. "Your scent drives me *crazy.*"

He was driving *her* crazy. It hadn't been like this before. With Lane, the passion had been slow to build. She'd been hesitant, unsure.

There was no room for uncertainty with Cooper. He swept her up into a storm of need. Pleasure already pulsed through her. She wanted him naked. Wanted to wrap her body around him and hold on as tight as she could.

He'd gotten rid of her bra. Those fast fingers of his. His mouth closed around one breast, and desire pierced through her. She curled her legs around his hips.

She hated not being able to touch his skin, so Gabrielle yanked up his shirt.

He helped her toss it across the room. Heat radiated off him. Those hard, rippling muscles. So much power. But he was always so careful with her. So very careful.

And he was making her wait. *"Cooper..."*

His hand was at the snap of her jeans. The snap popped free, and her zipper hissed down. Then his fingers were pushing inside the material. Pleasure wasn't just close. He stroked her, caressing her sensitive folds. His fingers drove into her. Pleasure exploded within her at his touch. She jerked against him, caught off guard by the fast rush of her release.

"You're so damned beautiful." He carried her into the bedroom. The bed dipped beneath their weight. In moments, he'd finished stripping and their clothes were scattered across the floor.

He took care of the protection, then he came back toward her.

But this time, Gabrielle wanted her chance to explore him.

She pushed him back on the bed. Cooper hesitated, frowning at her.

She smiled at him, even as the desire rose once more. Bending forward, she put her knees on either side of Cooper's body. Her mouth pressed to his throat. When he groaned, and his hands flew up to hold her hips, Gabrielle knew that she'd just found Cooper's weak spot.

Her tongue licked over his skin. Then she slid down. She explored his chest. Those muscles that just begged to be—

Licked.

She kissed his scars. Gabrielle hated the pain that Cooper had suffered, and as she felt those scars with her fingers and lips, she realized just how close he truly had come to death.

What if he'd really died on that mission? What if I'd never met him?

Her eyes squeezed shut. She didn't want to

think of a world without him. He'd come to mean so much to her, so quickly.

She placed another kiss on his scar, on the one right above his hip. Her fingers slid down—

"Enough!" The word was growled. He tumbled her onto her back. Positioned himself between her legs. "Sweetheart, I can't take any more."

His fingers threaded through hers as he thrust into her.

She'd found release moments before, but the instant he drove into her, that wonderful friction from his body had her tensing.

Eagerly, she met him. Thrust for thrust. The need spiraled and built. The desire beat between them.

There were no more words. She didn't have the breath to talk. Their lovemaking was fast and raw and consuming.

Her hips rose to meet him. Her heart raced.

When her release hit her, Gabrielle's whole body tightened. The pleasure was so intense—rolling over her in endless waves.

Cooper kissed her. He shuddered against her then drove into her core once more.

A tear leaked from the corner of her eye. Nothing had been like that for her before.

Moments passed, and the only sound she heard was the ragged catch of their breaths.

Finally, Cooper's head lifted. His eyes held

hers. "The case has nothing to do with what is happening between us. Right here, right now, it's only about you and it's about me."

She wished that things could stay this way.

Because as she gazed up at him, cloaked in the shadows of the room. Gabrielle realized just why his betrayal had hurt her so much.

And why, even despite the secrets he'd kept, she hadn't been able to turn away from him.

I'm falling in love with Cooper.

No, not falling.

She was already in love with her secret agent.

His mouth pressed to her cheek. He kissed the tear that she'd shed. And then he held her close.

Fear snaked through her because she liked the way his arms felt around her. She liked it too much.

The case had brought him to her.

Would the case also take him away?

RACHAEL MANCINI WAS exhausted. She'd just pulled a twenty-hour shift at the EOD's headquarters, and she was due back on duty at 0900. She shut her apartment door behind her, threw the lock and seriously thought about collapsing right there.

Into a very unglamorous puddle on her floor.

She lifted a weary hand and raked it through her hair. She'd crash in bed. After all, she was about 50 percent sure she could make it to the bedroom. After a few hours of refueling, she'd meet up with Dylan again.

He'd dropped her off, and the team leader had said he'd be back to pick her up so they could head in to the EOD together.

She shuffled away from the door.

Ten minutes later, she was just climbing into the haven of her bed when she heard knocking.

What the hell? She glanced at her clock. *No one* should be coming to her place at this hour.

Rachel grabbed her gun and padded, barefoot, for the door. She glanced through the peephole.

The Dragon waited on the other side of that door.

Her hands trembled around the weapon.

Thomas "Dragon" Anthony was a martial arts expert. He'd worked with the EOD since she'd been brought on board. The guy was quiet, dangerous—and he made her nervous. She'd heard too many tales about just how deadly he could be.

In the EOD, *all* of the agents were lethal. But Thomas was in a category all by himself.

She curled her fingers around the weapon and opened the door a few inches. Rachel kept her security chain in place, not that it would do any good at keeping someone like Thomas out.

Not if he wanted in.

"What are you doing here?" Rachel demanded as she kept her gun close.

His golden eyes glittered at her. "I was worried about you. I heard about the profile that's developing for the killer."

A profile that indicated the rogue was going after couples, killing one victim to make the other weaker.

"You don't need to worry about me." She and Thomas weren't close. Actually, as far as she knew, *no one* was close to the Dragon. He didn't let anyone close. But…

She'd saved his life. On a mission in the Middle East, Rachel had been on the team that pulled Thomas out of his prison. Sure, his captors had been dead by the time she arrived—courtesy of a weaponless Thomas—but he'd been bleeding out from the wounds he'd sustained.

She'd put pressure on the worst wound, had *kept* that wound closed all during the rough flight to freedom.

Not that Thomas knew about what she'd done. He'd lost consciousness right after takeoff.

"I think you and Dylan could be the next targets," Thomas said. His voice was deep, rumbling, and completely without any accent.

She blinked at his words, and she made sure her grip on the weapon remained steady. Thomas couldn't see her gun, but if he made a move toward her, she'd have it up in an instant.

After what had happened to the other EOD deaths, she wasn't going to trust anyone—

Except Dylan.

"You're wrong," she heard herself say. "We aren't a couple. We wouldn't come up on the guy's radar."

Thomas shook his head. "I see, so others see. I wanted to warn you."

Adrenaline pumped through her. She wasn't exactly feeling sleepy any longer. "You could have just called me."

His hands were fisted. A show of emotion, unusual for Thomas. "They're going to think it's me," he said softly.

Alarms were going off in her head.

"I lost her...my second mission. I lost her, and when the profiler digs through our files, she's going to think it's me." His breath heaved out. "It isn't."

"You need to talk to Noelle—"

"Warning you was priority."

But why hadn't he *called?*

His eyes glittered at her. "Can I come in?"

No way. "We can talk in the morning." They just had a bit of the waning night left. "I'll be at headquarters by 0900."

He leaned toward her. "You have to be careful—"

Rachel lifted her gun. "I am."

Every minute. Every moment.

"I'm going to ask you again," Rachel murmured. "Why didn't you just call me?"

He blinked. "I did. You didn't answer. That's why I was so worried. You fit the rogue's profile—I had to warn you."

She didn't buy his story. "You warned me. Now, we'll talk more tomorrow." Her immediate plans included a fast and frantic late-night call to Dylan. He needed to know about this little visit.

Thomas nodded. "Stay safe, Mancini." After one more long look at her, he turned away.

She didn't move. Not until she saw him head down the stairs.

Then she locked her door. Double-checked those locks. She put the gun down on the end table and hurried back into her bedroom to find her phone.

She grabbed it from her purse. Of course, it was working, it was—

Dead.

Rachel frowned. She'd charged the phone earlier. It should be fine. Damn it. She needed to contact Dylan, but she didn't have a landline, just her cell.

The floor creaked behind her.

Rachel froze.

She knew every inch of her apartment and just where to step for those familiar creaks and squeaks to sound. Because she knew the place so well, Rachel realized that someone was standing five feet behind her. Right inside the doorway.

The lights flashed off in her bedroom.

She didn't waste time screaming. Rachel turned and went in for the attack.

Chapter Eleven

Dylan Foxx knew that he shouldn't be hanging around Rachel's place.

He was starting to hit stalker territory.

He'd dropped her off thirty minutes ago. He'd left...but come back.

He'd learned about the profile that Agent Evers was working up—she thought the rogue was attacking couples. Eliminating the woman first then going after her lover.

That profile had made him worried.

He and Rachel weren't lovers, but...

...but I wish we were.

He'd wanted Rachel for years. Keeping his distance from her was impossible for him. He knew that he was too protective of her, that he got too close whenever she was near.

What if someone else had noticed that closeness, too?

What if the desire he felt for her caused Rachel to be put in danger?

His growing fear had driven him back to her place. It had made him lurk in the shadows of her apartment because he couldn't shake the feeling that something wasn't right.

He looked down at his phone. Maybe he should give her a call, just in case.

Then he heard the sound of footsteps coming quickly toward him.

He glanced up. The moonlight showed him the face of the man approaching—a familiar face.

Thomas Anthony.

In an instant, Dylan had grabbed the other man, jerking him to a stop. "What the hell are you doing here?" Dylan demanded.

He had his gun at the other man's throat.

Thomas stilled. "Easy..."

"Don't 'easy' me," Dylan snarled right back. Easy was the last thing he felt. "Why the hell are you coming out of Rachel's building at this damn time?"

The streetlight fell on Thomas's face. "That's why," he murmured. "I know how you feel, and I thought the killer might, too. I came to warn her."

Dylan thought he might be looking at the killer. Keeping his gun in place, he yanked up his phone with his left hand. He pressed the screen, instantly calling for Rachel.

"You're not going to get her," Thomas told him. "Her phone isn't working."

Rachel wasn't picking up.

He glanced up at her apartment on the top floor—the one on the far left end. All of her lights were off.

His back teeth ground together. "If you've hurt her…"

You're a dead man.

He wasn't scared of Thomas Anthony. No matter what stories circulated about the so-called Dragon, Dylan didn't care. He'd take the man down in an instant.

And if Thomas had hurt Rachel…*I'll tear him apart.*

"We're going upstairs," Dylan snapped. He'd see for himself that Rachel was fine.

Thomas turned around and headed toward the building. Dylan kept his gun at the man's back. They knew the rogue was EOD, and Thomas—an EOD agent with a shady past—*happened* to be at Rachel's place? To warn her? No way was he buying that story.

"I just left her," Thomas said. "She was very much alive, I assure you."

They climbed the stairs. No one else stirred in the apartment building.

Dylan's hands were sweating. He'd been in every hellhole on earth during his time as a SEAL, and he'd been coolly calm during every single mission. Yet as he hurried toward Rachel's apartment, his stomach knotted and fear thickened his blood.

A few more steps and they were at her apartment. He pounded on the door.

No sound emerged from inside Rachel's home.

He reached for the knob. *Locked.*

"Rachel!" He called out her name. Her neighbors could just get angry with him for yelling. He had to see her. "Open the door!"

But there was still no response.

"Something's wrong," Thomas said. Fear flashed across his face. "She came to the door within minutes when I was here before."

Dylan lifted his foot and kicked that door in.

He ran inside. "Rachel!"

A faint moan reached his ears.

He tore through the house, flying to her bedroom. It was pitch-black in there. He hit the light switch.

Dylan saw her crumpled on the floor. Blood was all around her. She was so still. So still.

"No!" The roar burst from him, and, in the next instant, he was on his knees beside her. With shaking hands he turned Rachel over. Her dark hair fell over his arm.

Blood.

"She fought him," Thomas muttered from behind Dylan. "Not like the others. She had a chance to fight for her life."

There were stab wounds on her chest, defensive wounds on her arms. And Dylan was afraid that she would die in his arms.

He yanked up his weapon, but didn't let her go. "You did this," he said as he took aim at the Dragon.

Thomas had his hands in front of him. No weapon, but that didn't mean the guy wasn't carrying a bloody knife. "It wasn't me, I swear! I came to warn her, just like I said before." He inched forward. "Let me help her. She helped me once, saved my life..."

"Take another step, and you'll have a bullet in your brain."

Rachel's blood was on his hands. Rachel was *dying* in his arms.

"I didn't do this," Thomas told him. "The apartment was locked from the inside."

And her bedroom window was wide open.

"I came out the front," Thomas continued doggedly. "I was with you, but whoever did this, *he's* getting away."

Thomas started to advance toward them.

Dylan fired his weapon.

THE RINGING PHONE woke Cooper, yanking him from a dream. He'd been running in that dream, desperately trying to get close to Gabrielle.

The loud ringing came again, and his eyes snapped open. The dream vanished.

Gabrielle was in his arms. *Safe.*

And the phone wasn't stopping.

"Cooper?" Her voice was husky, sexy. "Has something happened?"

A call at this hour *had* to mean something had gone wrong. He grabbed for the phone. "Marshall."

There was a murmur of voices. Then, "Rachel's hurt. The rogue went after her. *Her.*" Dylan's voice shook.

"She's alive." Cooper worried his clenched grip would shatter the phone. But Dylan had said *hurt,* not *dead.*

"Barely," was Dylan's low whisper. "We're in the ER, and I'm not leaving her. I found Thomas Anthony at her place."

The Dragon?

"She's bad," Dylan told him, and Cooper heard the pain and fear in the other man's voice. "I'm not sure she'll make it—"

"I'm on my way," Cooper promised.

"No! Don't come here—get to the EOD. Mercer took Thomas in for questioning after I shot the bastard."

Wait—Dylan had shot him?

"Get to the EOD." Dylan's voice grated over

the line. "Find out the truth. Thomas swore he was innocent—"

But obviously Dylan hadn't bought that story, or he wouldn't have shot the guy.

"Prove his innocence or prove his guilt," Dylan ordered.

Cooper looked to the left. He found Gabrielle's wide eyes on him. "I will." He ended the call and just stared at Gabrielle for a moment.

"What is it?" Worry shone in her eyes.

Cooper swallowed. "We were wrong about you being the next target. The rogue attacked Rachel."

She inhaled on a sharp gasp.

"She's alive, but Dylan said she's badly hurt." He didn't tell her that Dylan wasn't sure if Rachel would survive.

She has to survive.

If she didn't, Cooper wasn't sure how Dylan would react.

He climbed from the bed and grabbed his clothes. "There's a suspect in custody at the EOD. I'm going down for an interrogation."

"And I'm coming with you." She jumped out of bed, giving him one fine view of her body before she started yanking on clothes.

He hesitated. "Gabrielle, you know I can't just take you to the EOD office."

She shoved back her hair. "Then blindfold me. Do whatever you have to do." Gabrielle walked toward him with her gaze snapping. "But you aren't leaving me behind, *partner.*"

No, a partner wouldn't leave her behind.

He caught the back of her head and pulled her toward him. He kissed her, hard, fast and frantic, because he had to.

He knew Dylan must be in sheer hell right then.

And the thought of something like that happening to Gabrielle, of someone hurting her…

"Damn straight you're coming with me," he said.

Twenty-four seven. That had been their deal. He wasn't going to break any more promises to Gabrielle. He needed her to know that she could count on him.

For now.

Forever.

Cooper didn't plan on leaving her when the mission was over. He'd found something special with Gabrielle, and he wasn't about to let her go.

She gave him a little nod. He finished dressing and grabbed his gun, then his fingers twined with hers.

He hurried to the door, yanked it open.

And found Deuce standing there. Deuce nodded when he saw Cooper. The guy gave Gabrielle a wan smile. "I'm here for guard duty," he said with a little shrug.

Cooper frowned at him. "What?"

"You're wanted at headquarters." Now Deuce

was the one who frowned. "Didn't Dylan call you? Hell, I know he was messed up about Rachel, but Mercer wanted you to come in—"

"—for the interrogation," Cooper finished. "I know, we're going there now."

Deuce shook his head. "No, *you're* going." He glanced at Gabrielle. "Sorry, ma'am, but your clearance isn't high enough. The big boss sent me over to keep an eye on you until Cooper gets back."

Gabrielle stiffened. "Clearance or no clearance, I'm going with Cooper."

A long sigh came from Deuce. "Civilians never understand, do they, Coop?" He rolled back his shoulders. "Want me to give you two some privacy while you explain things to her? Make it fast, though, okay, buddy? Mercer isn't exactly patient."

Cooper hesitated.

"She'll be waiting when you come back," Deuce said as he turned away. "You know it. They're always waiting…"

No, they weren't. Sometimes you turned away—for a mission, for just a moment, and you looked back, and the one you loved was gone.

Loved.

His chest ached as Cooper stared down at Gabrielle. When had he started to love her? He hadn't loved anyone, or anything, not since he'd lost his mother.

Gone, in an instant.

The back of his hand brushed over Gabrielle's cheek.

"Cooper?" She gazed at him, waiting.

Did she think he'd leave her? That he'd break his promise to her?

"I want you to trust me," he said softly, needing her to understand. "I gave you my word. I won't go back on it, not ever again." Then he raised his voice, making sure Deuce could hear him as he said, "I'll call Mercer and let him know—"

The bullet hit Cooper, driving into his side and tearing through his body. Gabrielle screamed even as Cooper felt his body falling.

"You should've just left her," Deuce snapped. "Then I could have taken you out, one at a time, all nice and slow, just like I planned."

Cooper tried to pull his gun from the holster. Blood pumped from him, soaking the floor.

"Cooper!" Gabrielle reached for him.

He jerked out his weapon.

But Cooper didn't get the chance to fire that weapon. Because Deuce grabbed Gabrielle, and the man who'd worked side by side with Cooper pressed his gun to Gabrielle's temple.

"I don't like using a gun for my kills." Deuce's voice was low and hard, with a lethal edge. "It's just not personal enough. Death should be personal, don't you think?"

Cooper dragged himself to his feet. The bullet was still in him, and the wound burned as the blood dripped down his body.

He stared into Deuce's eyes.

Deuce smiled. "If you don't drop your weapon, I'll kill her right now."

Cooper let his weapon fall.

"Good," Deuce praised. The fingers of his left hand were wrapped tightly around Gabrielle's throat. Too tightly. "Now walk back into your apartment. Nice and slow."

Keeping his eyes on Deuce and ignoring the pain, Cooper retreated, walking backward into his apartment.

Deuce followed, still with that tight grip on Gabrielle. When they were all inside Cooper's place, Deuce told Gabrielle, "Lock the door. We want to make sure we don't have any unwanted guests."

Cooper saw her fingers tremble as she obeyed.

He could barely contain his fury—and his fear. Deuce had been the one to kill Lockwood? McAdams? The one to attack Rachel?

"You know, perhaps I've been wrong all this time..." Now Deuce's voice was considering. Mild and calm—just the way the guy was when they were playing cards.

Only this wasn't some card game.

This was life. Gabrielle's life.

"I thought it was better to kill the women they loved, then let the agents suffer until I put them out of their misery." Deuce thrust the gun barrel harder against Gabrielle's temple. "But making you *watch* while I kill her, oh, I think that is going to be even better..."

MERCER GLARED AT Thomas Anthony. The agent was wounded, but they'd patched him up.

For the moment.

If Mercer found out that Thomas was the rogue in his group, he'd do more than just wound the guy.

I'll destroy him.

"I'm not changing my story, Mercer," Thomas said. The guy's voice was even. No sign of rage or fear darkened his face. "I went to warn Rachel because I thought she was a target. When I left her, she was *fine*."

"And why'd you think she was a target? That part, I just don't see..."

"Rachel hauled me out of that prison camp. She stayed with me, telling me I had to fight, that I had to live, for nearly eight hours straight." Thomas stared steadily back at Mercer. "I heard the docs saying I was a dead man. And I heard her—telling me to live. The way I figure it, I owed her."

Mercer let his brows climb. "You owed her a knife to the chest? That was your way of saying thanks?"

Thomas's jaw tightened. "I owed her protection. When I heard about the profiler's theory, I knew I had to warn Rachel."

"Because you're in love with her..." He tossed this out, looking for a reaction from the agent.

"*No.* Because *Dylan Foxx* is. Why the hell else do you think the guy shot me? When he saw Rachel like that, on the floor and bleeding, he went crazy."

Mercer was well aware of Dylan's feelings for Rachel Mancini; he just wanted to see what Thomas would reveal.

"I was trying to help her." Thomas was repeating the same story, again and again. "Dylan thought I was attacking again, so he shot me. He wasn't about to let anyone but the doctors get close to his lady."

Mercer's eyes narrowed. "I find myself curious...just how did you learn of the profile that Agent Evers was developing? That profile *should* have been confidential."

Thomas shrugged. "Deuce told me about it. He said he'd heard the FBI agent talking to you."

Deuce?

Mercer kept his expression blank.

"Deuce said it looked like the killer was going

after the people that the agents cared about, attacking the women they loved first, then taking out the agents." Thomas rocked forward in his chair. "That's when I thought of Rachel. I knew about how Dylan felt—hell, how could I not? Have you *seen* the way the guy watches her? And I thought, hell, if the rogue wants to hurt the EOD, he'd focus on them. He'd take out two agents all at once."

Only the rogue hadn't been able to take out Rachel. She'd fought back.

The rogue had been denied his victim.

Would he try to attack her again? Or would he focus on someone else?

Mercer stood and advanced toward the door.

"You believe me, right?" Thomas called out. "Mercer?"

Mercer didn't respond. He went into the observation room. Two other agents were there—agents whom he trusted: Gunner Ortez and Logan Quinn. "I want to know where Deuce Porter is," Mercer said. "And I want to know *now*."

RACHEL'S EYELIDS TWITCHED. A soft moan slipped from her lips.

Dylan's heart raced in his chest. "It's okay," he told her, aware that his voice was no more than a rough rasp of sound. "You're safe." She was headed into the OR. She shouldn't even be opening her eyes then.

Not with the drugs that the doctors had given her.

But Rachel was staring up at him. Fear and fury battled in her stare. "D-D…"

"Take it easy," he told her. "I won't let anyone hurt you. Not ever again."

She grabbed for his hand. Her grip was surprisingly strong. *"Deuce…"*

And as understanding sank into Dylan, her rage became his.

"WHY?" COOPER GROWLED. He kept his eyes on Deuce. If he looked at Gabrielle, if he saw her fear, he was afraid he'd lose control.

Deuce was hurting her. And Cooper knew that unless he stopped him, Deuce would take pleasure in killing Gabrielle.

That can't happen. Cooper didn't want to live in a world that didn't contain Gabrielle.

She was too important.

She was everything.

"Vivian," Deuce said softly. "My beautiful Vivian. She's why." He lifted the gun a few inches from Gabrielle's temple.

That's right. Get the gun off her. Focus on me.

"Do you remember her, Coop? You'd just joined the EOD on that mission."

Cooper's guts were twisted in knots. *Vivian. 'ivian Donaldson.* "She was the blonde. She vas—"

"Mine!" Deuce screamed at him. The gun vent right back to Gabrielle's temple. "Vivian vas mine, and I was hers. We met in the Marines. Ve joined the EOD together. Our lives *were* to- ;ether." Deuce's breath heaved out. "Until that nission…that last damn mission that got screwed o hell and back."

"Did she die?" Gabrielle asked him softly.

"She jumped in front of me." Deuce was star- ng at Cooper, but Cooper wasn't sure the other nan actually saw him in that moment. "She took he gunfire meant for me. The bullets—they tore hrough her body. She jerked and shuddered, and he died." His breath heaved. "I was holding her n my arms, and more bullets came flying. They nit me. I *should* have died with her—"

"But we pulled you out," Cooper said. They'd ılso taken Vivian. They'd tried to help her, but it ıad been too late.

And, once he'd recovered, Aaron Porter had become Deuce. The moniker was both for the act that he could so easily assume the identity of another person…and because he'd been given a second chance.

A chance to kill?

"I lost her," Deuce whispered.

"So you wanted them to lose, too," Gabrielle said. She didn't sound afraid.

She sounded…sad.

Once again, that gun lifted from her head. "Why should they get the happy ending? The EOD *took* my life away. They didn't give me a second chance—they took her, and I had nothing." He smiled at Cooper. A chilling sight. "So I took from them. I took their hope. I let them see what it was like to have nothing, and then killed them."

Cooper took a careful step toward him. "They were your friends."

"They were the men who should have saved Vivian. *You* were one of those men. You were there, too. If you weren't going to save her, then you should have let me die with her!"

Deuce wasn't sane. Not any longer. Too much grief and pain had twisted him. Broken the man he'd been.

Cooper's phone began to ring, vibrating in his pocket.

"Don't!" Deuce yelled. "Don't even think of answering it."

The phone kept ringing.

"Vivian wouldn't want you doing this," Cooper told him, trying to reach the man that Deuce had been. Was Aaron even still in there? "She was in the EOD to help people, not to hurt them."

But Deuce laughed. “The EOD isn’t what you think. We’re just Bruce Mercer’s attack dogs, nothing more. Well, guess what? I’m attacking on my own. I’m getting my vengeance, and I’m showing the world what’s really going on…”

Gabrielle pulled at the hand around her neck. “V-Van didn’t leave that message in blood, did he?”

Another rough bark of laughter escaped from Deuce. “Now you’re seeing things. That was me. All *me*.”

“Because you wanted me to find out about the EOD,” she whispered. Cooper still couldn’t look in her eyes. He didn’t want to see her fear. His body tensed as he took another step forward. He had to get close enough to attack.

“You wanted me…to write a story on them, didn’t you?” Gabrielle’s words were distracting Deuce, and Cooper needed the man to stay distracted. Distracted prey was easier to take down.

“You were supposed to show the world…but you didn’t!” Spittle flew from Deuce’s mouth. “Everyone should have learned the truth. At the EOD, we’re all killers! They should fear *us*. But you didn’t write the story. You just let him—” He pointed the gun at Cooper. “You let him seduce you, and you buried the story!” Red stained Deuce’s cheeks, and, in the light of the apartment, Cooper could see the blood on the man’s hand.

Rachel's blood.

"He was using you," Deuce snapped. "You were the assignment."

Cooper took another step forward. "She's *not* an assignment."

Deuce's smile chilled Cooper's blood. "What is she, then? Why don't you tell us both?"

"You already know." That was why the bastard was there. Why he planned to hurt Gabrielle. "That's the way your game works, right? You take the ones that the agents love, so we feel your pain." He lifted his hands, acting as if he were no threat. "Don't do it, man. *Don't.* I can't imagine what you went through when Vivian died—"

"No, you *can't!*" Deuce yelled at him. "But you will. Now why don't you tell her that you love her before she dies?"

"Cooper?" Her voice was a soft rasp.

Finally, he looked at her. Because this was it. The last moment. And he wanted her to know how he felt, no matter what else happened.

"I love you." He wasn't sure when it had happened. When she'd first started to slip into his fantasies? When she'd come smiling, to his doorstep, offering him her chocolate chip cookies?

Or when he'd seen her choke back her fear—and work to get justice for those lost?

Hell, the when didn't matter.

He just knew he loved her.

He also knew that he'd die for her.

And he'd *kill* before he let anyone hurt her.

Her lips trembled. "Don't…*don't*—"

Her warning came too late because he was already moving as Deuce started turning the gun back toward Gabrielle. That gun was *not* getting to her temple again. He lunged forward. His body slammed into Deuce's even as his hands fought for the gun.

They tumbled to the floor. Deuce still had a grip on Gabrielle, even though she was fighting him. Cooper grabbed for the weapon—and the gun exploded.

Chapter Twelve

The gunshot echoed like thunder in her ears.

It reminded her of another time, another blood-soaked night.

A night when she'd lost another man that she loved.

Cooper groaned, and his body sagged back.

"You weren't supposed to be first," Deuce snarled as he lifted the gun and took aim at Cooper's prone form. "But if that's the way you want it, old buddy..."

"No!" Gabrielle threw her body forward and wrapped her arms around Cooper. There was so much blood. The scent filled her nose and had her stomach turning. Cooper's body was slack. And...cold. His usual warmth seemed to be fading, and that chill terrified her.

"Get away from him!" Deuce rose to his feet. "Now!"

If she moved, he'd shoot Cooper again.

She hunched her body over Cooper's. His eyes

vere closed. She wanted them open. She needed o look into his gaze once more. He'd said that ie loved her.

"I love you, too," she whispered, and tears had he words choking out of her. "I didn't… I didn't nean to love you, but it just happened." He'd gotten past her defenses. Gotten right to the heart that she'd tried to guard so carefully. "Don't do this, please, don't leave me."

"Don't worry." The gun pressed to her temple once more. "You'll be joining him soon enough."

Her head lifted, but she didn't move her body. She was half sprawled over Cooper, trying to shield him as much as she could. She gazed up at Deuce and saw a monster staring back at her. "Killing us won't give your Vivian any justice."

His lips tightened. "Revenge is better than justice any day of the week."

No, it wasn't. "I've done *nothing* to you! I didn't even know you until a few days ago."

"You've done nothing," he said, giving a little nod, "and you *are* nothing, to me." Then his gaze slid to Cooper. "But to him, you're everything."

She didn't have a weapon. His gun was jamming into her temple.

This was it, then.

Cooper was too badly hurt to help her. She didn't even think he was conscious.

She'd attack Deuce. She would fight—she would *try*. And if she failed, she'd die.

Her fingers squeezed Cooper's.

He didn't squeeze hers back, but his chest rose and fell. Cooper was still alive.

I'll keep him that way.

"It's over for you, Deuce," she said, speaking quickly. Distraction would be the key here. "Rachel survived your attack. She's at the hospital and she's going to tell everyone that you were the one hurting her—"

Cooper's phone rang again.

Gabrielle flinched.

Luckily, Deuce didn't. If he had, his trigger finger might have squeezed and she could have died right then.

"Th-that could be Dylan. He was at the hospital with her. I bet they already know you're the D.C. Striker."

"Doesn't matter," he told her, sounding too confident and not at all distracted. "You think I don't know how to vanish? I'll just reappear in another city, with another face, another name, and I'll keep hunting. I won't stop until I destroy the EOD agents. The EOD took away Vivian, and I'll make Mercer and his attack dogs *pay*."

Distract. Distract. "No one understands why you're doing this—the public just thinks you're a serial killer."

He grunted at that.

She licked her lips. "I can help you to make them all understand."

The pressure of the gun's barrel eased. "That's what you were *supposed* to do."

Keep him talking. "It's what I will do. L-let me get to a computer. I can write your story. I can publish it. I can make everyone understand about the EOD and what they cost you." If he'd just back away from Cooper, then she'd be able to breathe easier.

Getting him away from Cooper was priority one. Getting that gun away from her head? A definite priority number two for her.

"Yeah, yeah, they need to know," Deuce muttered. His eyes had narrowed to slits. "We're gonna tell them." He grabbed her arm and yanked her to her feet.

Then he drew back his foot and kicked Cooper as hard as he could, right in the wound on Cooper's side.

"No!" Gabrielle screamed.

Cooper didn't move.

"He's already dead," Deuce said and there was satisfaction on his face. "His heart just doesn't know it yet. A few more pumps, and he's gone." Then, seemingly certain that Cooper wasn't going to trouble him, he started pulling Gabrielle toward Cooper's computer.

The gun wasn't at her head.

And Cooper *wasn't* already dead.

His phone stopped ringing.

"Come on," Deuce demanded as he yanked harder on her arm. "It's time for the world to know—"

The front door smashed in.

Deuce whirled toward that door, shouting, and Gabrielle used that moment—*distraction!*—to slam into him as hard as she could. He staggered back, and tripped over Cooper's end table. He crashed to the floor, and, as he fell, Deuce yanked her down with him.

The gun flew from his fingers. Gabrielle scrambled for it, but he caught her around the waist and hauled her back against him. He flipped her over and his hands went right to her throat.

"Let her go."

That low, lethal voice came from just a few feet away. Deuce didn't let her go, but he turned his head and stared up at the man who'd just kicked in the door.

The EOD director—the guy Cooper had called Mercer—stood there, with a gun in his hand. A gun that was trained right on Deuce.

"I gave you an order," Mercer barked. "Get your hands off her and get to your feet, *now.*"

Deuce slowly freed her, and Gabrielle sucked

in desperate gulps of air. Spots danced around her eyes.

"I didn't expect you to come," Deuce drawled. His hands weren't on Gabrielle's throat, but he hadn't moved back, either. Actually, his hand was dipping toward his waistband. "I mean, the big boss doesn't usually get his hands dirty."

"I made an exception this time." Mercer had a dead aim at the man's head. But even though Gabrielle saw that his aim hadn't wavered, Mercer's attention had. His gaze was on Cooper.

Deuce laughed. "You've always been making exceptions for him. You think I didn't notice? Hell, from the very beginning…that rescue mission was a suicide job, but you still sent us out to find him. You were desperate to get some jumper out of that hellhole, and I had to wonder…*why?*"

"I value all of my agents—"

"He wasn't an agent then," Deuce pointed out. "Not then, but you risked our lives for him."

Mercer was still looking at Cooper. A mistake. "Mercer!" She yelled her warning.

His gaze swung back, but Deuce had already pulled a backup weapon from his ankle holster. Deuce didn't hesitate—he fired on the director.

Even as Mercer fired at him.

The thunder blasted in Gabrielle's ears. Blood bloomed on Mercer's chest, and he staggered back.

Deuce fell to his knees. He'd been hit, too, and

the blood covered his chest just as surely as it covered Mercer's.

But Deuce wasn't done. He turned his head, stared at her. Stared, smiled, and lifted his gun.

They were inches apart.

I won't go out without a fight.

"No!" A deep cry of fury and fear. Not her cry. Cooper's.

And—Cooper was there. He lunged at Deuce, with a knife gripped tightly in his hand.

Deuce tried to spin toward the new threat, but Cooper had moved too swiftly. Cooper attacked with his knife, driving it into Deuce's body.

Gunfire didn't thunder again.

The gun fell to the floor. Deuce gasped. His hands fought for the knife.

Cooper shoved it even deeper into Deuce's chest. "It's…over…" Cooper growled. "Over."

And it was.

Gabrielle grabbed the gun. She pointed it right at Deuce.

But Deuce wasn't looking at her. Blood soaked the floor beneath him, and he lay there, staring at nothing.

Not anymore.

His gaze was open. Empty.

Gone.

"G-Gabrielle…" Cooper reached her for her.

Her wonderful, strong, *alive* Cooper. She hugged him and held on to him as tightly as she could.

More footsteps raced into the room.

"Mercer?" she heard one man demand sharply.

She didn't look over at the new arrivals. She was too busy holding tight to Cooper.

"I'm…fine," Mercer told them. "Get Cooper—he needs…hospital…"

Cooper was sagging in her arms. "Cooper?" Tears slipped from her eyes. No, no, he couldn't do this. The killer was dead. This was the point where everyone was supposed to be okay.

But Cooper was too pale. His clothes were soaked in blood, and he was so cold.

Too cold.

She held him, as tightly as she could.

When the EMTs rushed in, she was there.

So was Mercer.

Mercer's body trembled, but he glared at the EMTs. "You keep him alive. Keep him *alive*."

"And you damn well better follow his orders!" Gabrielle heard herself shout. Tears thickened her voice.

"Annalise's son won't go out like this. He won't," Mercer vowed.

Then they were in the ambulance rushing toward the hospital. Mercer was in the back of that ambulance with her. EMTs were trying to work on him and on Cooper, but Mercer kept shoving them away and demanding that they focus on Cooper's wounds.

"D-don't worry..." Cooper whispered.

She barely heard his words over the hum of the machines and the scream of the ambulance's siren.

"I'm not...leaving you," he said. His eyelids flickered then his eyes opened. The blue was hazy, weak, but he was looking straight at her. "Not...ever..."

"You'd better not," she told him, not able to hold back her tears. "Cooper, I've got plans for us. Do you hear me? Lots of plans. Spaghetti dinners and cherry pies and more breaking and entering. We're just getting started. I just found you." She could taste the salt of her own tears. "I don't want to lose you."

It almost looked as if he smiled. "Promise..." A bare breath of sound from him. "You won't."

He'd said that he wouldn't break any more promises to her. No more lies. No more secrets.

Only truth.

I won't lose him.

Hope began to grow inside of her.

Hope that her secret agent was as strong as she'd always thought. Strong enough to cheat death—and to stay with her.

Forever.

COOPER HATED BEING in the hospital. The place smelled too much of antiseptic, and the stark white walls hurt his eyes.

Not that the room was 100 percent white. To the left, right near his lone window, he had an explosion of color—twelve blue balloons, reaching for the ceiling.

The balloons were from Gabrielle.

His beautiful Gabrielle. She was beside him right then.

Sleeping.

She'd been with him since the attack.

He'd woken a few times, seen her staring at him with fear and hope in her gaze. One time when he'd fought through the drugs, he'd opened his eyes and seen her holding those balloons.

She'd been trying to smile at him then.

She'd been crying, too.

Her fingers were entwined with his. He curled his around hers a little more, squeezing lightly.

Gabrielle gave a little gasp, and her eyes immediately flew open. "Cooper?"

He smiled at her.

In the next instant, Gabrielle was *in* that bed with him. She put her mouth to his and kissed him.

He loved having her mouth on his.

Her kiss was light and gentle, and the woman

was out of her head if she thought that was enough to satisfy him. Her body was next to his, not touching him, and that wasn't good enough, either.

He pulled her closer, ignoring the burn of the IV in his arm.

"No!" Gabrielle said, pulling back. "You have to be careful. You need—"

"I have what…I need." He was staring right at her.

Her lips trembled.

"You said…you loved me…" His voice was raspy, and talking made his throat ache more, but he didn't care. The pain just meant that he was alive.

"I did," she whispered, searching his eyes.

"Say it again."

Her smile bloomed, full and beautiful. "I love you, Cooper Marshall."

"Again." His demand. He would never get tired of hearing those words from her.

Gabrielle pressed another too light kiss to his lips. "I love you."

This time, he was the one to tremble. Because, for an instant, he'd wondered what he would have done if Deuce *had* killed her.

I would have been lost.

"Cooper?"

He shoved the darkness away from his mind

and focused on the light—on Gabrielle. "I think we need…to reevaluate our partnership," he managed to tell her.

Her brows lifted. "We do?"

"Um, I was thinking about something more… permanent." A whole lot more permanent.

She shifted against him, pushing herself up so that she could gaze down at him. "That had better not be the drugs talking."

A rough laugh escaped from him. That was his Gabrielle. Only she could get to him—could make him laugh, make him dream of a future. "It's not. It's me." But then his gaze fell on the white box that was perched on the table near his bed. A small, square box.

The kind that usually stored jewelry.

Gabrielle followed his gaze. "Mercer brought that by for you. He said that he thought you'd be needing it." Her fingers stroked his arm, an almost absent gesture. He loved her touches. Her caresses.

Loved *her*.

"His wounds weren't nearly as bad as yours—no internal organs hit for him. He was cleared the next day, but you…" Her hand stilled on him. "You scared me."

He caught her fingers, brought them to his lips and pressed a hard kiss to her knuckles. "I'll do my…damnedest to never scare you again." He only wanted to make her happy.

Some of the sadness eased from her eyes. "Rachel's okay. She's still here, and Dylan's making sure that she gets plenty of rest."

Cooper suspected that Dylan was too worried about Rachel to let her out of his sight.

The little matter of a life-or-death situation could sure change a man's perspective.

It had certainly changed his.

Gabrielle climbed from the bed. She picked up the white box and handed it back to him.

Frowning, Cooper studied the box. He had no idea what Mercer could be giving to him. "About…our partnership," Cooper began as he opened the box.

But then he fell silent.

A ring was inside the box.

Not just any ring. A ring with two diamonds, and a twisted band of gold.

"Cooper?"

"This…this was my grandmother's ring." The memory was there, in the back of his mind. His grandmother had visited him when he'd been a kid, maybe four or five, and he'd seen that ring. He'd played with it, tracing the diamonds and that braided twist while he'd sat in his grandmother's lap. He'd never forgotten that ring.

Then his grandparents had died. His mother had died.

He'd never seen the ring again.

So what in the hell was Mercer doing with it?

"It wasn't an enemy who took her." Mercer's words seemed to whisper through his mind. *"Cancer did that. It came in an instant. It took her from me too soon. I blinked, and she was just—gone."*

His fingers closed around the ring. He saw the small note that had been folded and tucked in the bottom of the box.

Gabrielle was at his bedside, watching him silently.

I always want her at my side. Wherever I go, whatever I do, I want Gabrielle there.

He opened up that folded piece of paper. A brief note had been written there. *Annalise would want you to give this to the woman you love.*

That was all it said.

But then, those few words said everything.

"Cooper?"

He had to swallow twice in order to clear his throat. "I should...I should be on my knees for this." He tried to climb out of the hospital bed.

Since he was still weak, he pretty much *did* fall to his knees.

Gabrielle grabbed him and staggered beneath his weight. "What are you doing?"

"Trying to…" He made it. His knees touched down. "Trying to ask you about our partnership. I told you, I want one…that lasts forever." He lifted the ring toward her.

Her lips were parted. He waited for her to speak. Gabrielle always had plenty to say.

Only she wasn't speaking at that moment.

And she was scaring him.

The man who'd never known fear was about to shake again.

"Gabrielle?" Cooper prompted.

She blinked. "Y-you were just shot."

Cooper nodded.

"You've been unconscious for forty-eight hours."

He didn't know how long he'd been out. Cooper didn't think it mattered.

"You wake up, and the first thing you do…" She swiped her hand over her cheek. Oh, wait, was she *crying?* He'd so messed up the proposal. "The first thing you do is ask me to marry you?"

Again, he nodded. "I love you."

Her arms flew around his neck. "Forever," she whispered in his ear.

He curled his arm around her. The IV jerked loose. So what? *The pain means I'm alive—alive with the woman I love.* "Forever," he told her.

She kissed him.

He hoped that kiss meant yes.

Gabrielle slowly lifted her mouth from his. "I'll take that new partnership." She also took the ring. He helped slide it onto her ring finger. The diamonds gleamed.

A part of his past.

He looked into her eyes.

His future.

For a man who'd never looked beyond the next mission, life had sure changed. Because in that moment, when he gazed into Gabrielle's eyes, Cooper saw every dream he'd ever had.

Love.

A family.

A real home.

Every single thing he wanted—it was right there.

He was going to grab tight to those dreams. No one—nothing—would ever take them away.

Cooper kissed Gabrielle once more, and he knew that he was tasting paradise.

Epilogue

"You *can't* go in there!" Judith's voice snapped. "Mercer is busy! He can't be—"

His office door flew open.

Mercer leaned back in his seat and studied the man who'd just fought his way past Judith, Mercer's determined assistant. Judith was currently glaring at Cooper Marshall.

Cooper was glaring at Mercer.

Ah, life was back to normal.

"It's all right," Mercer said as he waved Judith back. "I was planning to talk with him."

Judith narrowed her eyes on Cooper. "You've made my list, Marshall."

Cooper blinked at that. Surprise flashed briefly over his face.

"I won't be forgetting this," she added, then stalked away.

The door slammed behind her.

Mercer put his hands flat on the desk. "You're

ooking better. For a while there, agent, I thought you weren't as strong as I—"

"My mother had a brother," Cooper cut through Mercer's words. "She said that he was in the military. That he was a soldier who saved lives."

Mercer's fingers began to tap on the desk.

"She told me all kinds of stories about him when I was growing up. Stories that made me want to be like him. Hell, those stories are the reason I joined the service. I wanted to make a difference, just like he'd done."

Mercer's gaze swept over Cooper's face. "You have."

"My mother…she said her brother died."

Mercer swallowed.

"But then…" Cooper looked out the window at the busy streets of D.C. "I died, too, didn't I? I thought my 'death' was so I could help the EOD, but there was more to that, right? You were trying to cover my past, trying to protect me."

"I don't know what—"

"Your daughter has to be under constant guard because you don't want your enemies getting to her. I figure all of those enemies would go after your nephew just as easily."

Mercer's fingers stopped tapping. "Yes, they would."

Cooper nodded. "My mother…she sure loved her brother. At the end, she called for him."

Mercer’s eyes burned.

“Just so you know,” Cooper murmured. “She wanted Ben. Her big brother, Benjamin.”

Benjamin Marshall. He’d been that man, in another life. Long before he’d become Bruce Mercer

“I loved her,” Mercer’s words were rough with emotion.

“I know you did.” Cooper took a step toward him. “You paid for my college. You’ve been the one in the background, all my life, watching me haven’t you?”

“Not all your life. I wasn’t there when Annalise needed me most.” His shoulders hunched at the memory.

Cooper walked around the desk. He put his hand on Mercer’s shoulder. “My mother loved you,” he said again. “And she wouldn’t want you blaming yourself for the way things ended.”

Annalise had been good. Such an open heart, a warm smile. “You have her eyes,” Mercer whispered.

Cooper’s hand tightened on his shoulder. “ gave Gabrielle the ring.”

Mercer nodded. “Annalise…she would have liked Gabrielle.” He found that he could smile “Gabrielle’s got a lot of fire in her. She’s not afraid of anything. Just like you.”

“Oh, I’m afraid,” Cooper surprised him by saying. “Because of Gabrielle, I’m terrified. I’m afraid that if I don't grab on to her, if I don't take my chance with her, I'll lose out on the best thing that could have ever happened to me."

Mercer glanced up at him. "Hold her tight. Fight like hell for her, and *never* let your enemies get close."

Cooper nodded. He lifted his hand and turned to walk away.

Mercer stood. The chair rolled back.

Cooper glanced over his shoulder.

"And...if you ever need me," Mercer managed to say, "I'm here. I—I know I'm not much, not in terms of..." He trailed off because he didn't know what to say.

Not in terms of family.

He'd been a shadow in Cooper's life for so long. Mercer knew he didn't have the right to ask for anything more.

Not that he could. Not really. He'd made sure that no one would ever be able to trace his blood link to Cooper. That protection was his gift to the man.

Not that he expected Cooper to believe that.

Not that he had the right to expect anything of Cooper Marshall.

But...Cooper hadn't left yet.

"Gabrielle and I are talking about a wedding in the fall. We have to, uh, wait for her boss to get back in town." Cooper's lips twisted. "Seems someone sent Hugh to the Cayman Islands, and seeing as how he's the one who will be giving away the bride, Gabrielle wants to make sure the guy's back."

"I can make sure of that," Mercer promised softly.

Cooper nodded, but he still didn't leave. "You know, when Gabrielle found out that I was an agent, she could've kicked me out of her life. Told me that I was a liar and just walked away from me." He paused. "She didn't. She gave me a second chance. She's letting me prove myself to her. I'm going to show her that there's a whole lot more to me than she thought."

Mercer's fingers had started to tap against the desktop once more.

"I believe in second chances," Cooper said. "Deuce didn't. *I do.*" Then he exhaled slowly. "So don't make me regret this but…you'll be invited to the wedding, too. I'd like to learn more about you. About the soldier my mom loved so much."

Mercer's hand lifted and rubbed against his chest. It wasn't his new wound that was aching.

It was something that went much deeper.

"Maybe you can tell me about her, too," Cooper continued softly. "Because I'd like to share those stories. I'll have kids one day. They should know about her."

"Yes," Mercer's voice was too rough. He couldn't help that. "They should."

One more nod and Cooper slipped away.

The door shut behind him.

Mercer closed his eyes for a moment. *You have a good son, Annalise.*

His eyes opened.

And I'll damn well be worth the second chance that he's giving me.

He'd prove himself to Cooper. After all, he'd never failed a mission. *I won't fail him.*

A knock sounded at his door. "Mercer," Judith called.

Judith hated using the intercom. It wasn't personal enough for her.

She opened the door and poked her head inside. "Dylan Foxx is here to see you." A pause, then, "*He* has an appointment."

Mercer inclined his head. "Send him in."

She turned away.

Speaking of missions...

Dylan Foxx stalked inside Mercer's office. One glance and Mercer knew Dylan was different. Rachel's attack had changed the man, just as Mercer had feared.

The news Mercer was about to give him wasn't going to help the situation. In fact, it might just push Foxx over the edge.

Mercer motioned to the seat before him. "I'm

afraid we have a problem," he said, as Dylan sat down.

Dylan stared back at him.

"It's seems Rachel Mancini's past isn't dead."

The agent turned to stone before him.

"And if we don't act to permanently bury that past, I'm afraid that Mancini will find herself in the crosshairs of a killer once more."

A muscle jerked along Dylan's jaw. "Tell me what I have to do."

Yes, that had rather been the response that Mercer expected.

He leaned forward and got to work.

* * * * *